APPLEBY
AND
HONEYBATH

APPLEBY
AND
HONEYBATH

MICHAEL INNES

Dodd, Mead & Company
New York

Published by Dodd, Mead & Company, Inc.
79 Madison Avenue, New York, N.Y. 10016

Distributed in Canada by
McClelland and Stewart Limited, Toronto

Manufactured in the United States of America

FIRST EDITION

Library of Congress Cataloging in Publication Data

Innes, Michael, 1906–
Appleby and Honeybath.

I. Title.
PR6037.T466A85   1983   823'.912   83-11565
ISBN 0-396-08247-5

APPLEBY
AND
HONEYBATH

1

THE AFFAIR MAY BE SAID TO HAVE STARTED, AS CHARLES
Honeybath's adventures were apt to do, with his engaging
to paint a portrait. But more exactly, it started when he
found the body in the library. Whose body it was, and how
it had come there, and why, and when: these were matters
for some time to be much in doubt. But it may be stated at
once that the library was the least frequented room in the
house, and therefore of obvious convenience for unobtrusively storing a corpse. Honeybath himself had gone into
the place only on an impulse so merely whimsical that he
found it embarrassing to explain even to John Appleby,
although the men were old friends.

The portrait was to be of a certain Terence Grinton, a
red-faced man in robust middle age, who described himself
in Who's Who as a landed proprietor, and for whom pursu-
ing foxes over the length and breadth of two counties might
fairly be described as a variety of religious experience. The
portrait was being subscribed for by his fellow Nimrods and
Jorrockses in recognition of the fact that for donkeys' (or
hunters') ages he had sustained the role of M. F. H. at
considerable expense to himself.

The subscribers, who had perhaps slightly old-fashioned

1

ideas on what they might dictate to a Royal Academician, had stipulated that there should be no nonsense about the thing: old Terry must be in a pink coat and wearing his topper. Honeybath had agreed at once. The combination of hunting pink and sanguine complexion (which is common enough) was a problem that interested him.

There had been some question of Terry being depicted as sitting, or standing beside, a horse. But Honeybath had made it clear that a horse is very expensive. A horse, in fact, is as expensive as a man, so the commission would have been virtually for two portraits. With a favourite groom thrown in it would be classifiable as a conversation piece, and so cost the earth. The subscribers didn't feel up to that sort of a bill.

Grinton seldom went to London, so attendance in the artist's studio wasn't on. Honeybath had therefore agreed to do most of the work while being put up at Grinton Hall as a guest. His first idea was to give this open air man a *plein air* setting; to have a blowy kind of world around him and the Hall itself in a middle distance. But Grinton felt that this would draw attention to the absence of a horse, and thus asperse the liberality of his friends, who had set up the project in the first place. So it had to be indoors, in one fashion or another.

It was at this point that Honeybath, already staying at Grinton and becoming a shade impatient about the whole arrangement, began to amuse himself with bits of fun. He thought of a window embrasure, flanked by imposing pilasters, and improbably draped with enormous curtains, abundantly tasselled, and in whatever red-inclining-to-orange would be trickiest with that complexion and those togs. He discussed this rather technically with Lady Appleby, who was in some sort of cousinship with the Grintons and had insisted on taking her husband to a long weekend at Grinton. As Judith Appleby was a sculptor (only she still liked to say "sculptress"), she was not all that interested in colours and hues. But she liked talking to Honeybath.

Then Honeybath had another idea. His last job had been providing a Cambridge college with a likeness of his Master, who was an eminent theologian. Very properly, Honeybath had posed this scholar in his study and against a background of calf-and-vellum-bound patristic learning rising from floor to ceiling. The books were all outsize folios, and bulky at that. They looked as if they had come into being at the hands of Johann Guttenberg in Mainz round about the middle of the fifteenth century and had been putting on weight ever since. To this towering burden of learning Honeybath had imparted a minute forward tilt, imperceptible in itself to other than a trained eye, but sufficient to create an uneasy impression that the Master was at some considerable risk of erudite entombment as he sat at his desk.

Recalling this episode now, Honeybath also recalled having been told about the Grinton library. He hadn't been invited to take a look at it, and it was his impression that it existed on the fringes of the Grinton family mind as a slightly uncomfortable joke. According to Judith Appleby, scholarship had raised its incomprehensible head every now and then—perhaps every third or fourth generation— among the normally normal Grintons. There had been Thomas Sackville Grinton who, in the last years of the First Elizabeth, had assisted Philemon Holland in his translation of the *Historia Naturalis* of the Elder Pliny. There had been Jonathan Grinton, author of a book mysteriously entitled *Divers Private Recreations*, which was published in

1715 but of which no copy was known to be extant. Jonathan had both philosophic and literary friends, and was believed to have entertained at Grinton somebody referred to by Terence Grinton as "a little chappie called Pope." And so on.

Thus the library, considered as a collection of books, didn't come quite to a stop until well into the Victorian period. But the ghost of the library (if the expression isn't too strange a one) was somehow at large at Grinton. This was perhaps because Mr. Grinton wasn't merely of a philistine temperament and indifferent to books. He hated them, particularly if their authors had names like Pliny or Julius Caesar. He remembered the beaks at his public school, he used to say, trying to beat the bloody things into his backside. And enough had been enough. This may suggest that Terence Grinton must have been accounted disagreeable by civilized or cultivated persons. But it wasn't so. His wife, Dolly Grinton, who had quite different ideas, often filled the house with acquaintances of lively (and sometimes eccentric) intellectual and artistic interests. And most of these quite took to the squire. (When they referred to their host thus, or even so addressed him, they thought of themselves as being mildly facetious. But this shade of implication never crossed Terence's own mind.)

No more than Charles Honeybath had any of these visitors, so far as was known, ever been invited to view the library. A housemaid did some dusting in it once a week, and every two or three years Terence Grinton, when the hunting season was over and he had taken his family briefly on holiday, arranged that this and other apartments should have a "go through" at the hands of a firm of contractors. There were servants at Grinton, but nowadays they were intermittently in short supply.

4

However, the corpse has already been waiting for us too long.

What was prompting Honeybath when he came on it was, as has been said, a mere whim—little more than a velleity, to use a learned word. With that portrait of the Master of a College in his mind, there came to him the amusing idea of posing a Master of Fox Hounds, all dressed up for the chase, similarly before an imposing stack of his own bibliophilic possessions. The Cambridge portrait had yet to be exhibited at the Academy; it might be possible to persuade the hanging committee to find a place for Terence Grinton thus conceived not next to it, indeed, since that would be a trifle crude, but not too far away. A good deal of quiet mirth would be thus occasioned. Needless to say, this was all absolute nonsense. Even if Grinton could be persuaded to such a pose, which was extremely unlikely, one couldn't make a monkey of the man after such a fashion. Nevertheless the mere idea *was* amusing. And it was what moved Charles Honeybath to take a peep into that library.

It wasn't, of course, kept under lock and key. There just seemed to be an unspoken understanding that it wasn't among the ground-floor rooms, fairly numerous in such a house, through which guests might wander at will. Quite commonly there is such a room, called a study, an office, a book room or whatever, reserved for the private use of the owner. But as Grinton himself never entered his library, this convention clearly didn't apply. Honeybath told himself that the apartment, obviously of considerable size, was demonstrably what house agents call a "reception" room, and that he could scarcely be charged with violating his host's hospitality if he went in and glanced round it.

His first impression was that somebody else had been

taken with the same idea, and had signalled his approval of the library and its appointments by sitting down comfortably in an armchair in the middle of it. And Honeybath, perhaps because already possessed by a slight consciousness of intruding where he had no business, was momentarily confused to the extent of exclaiming, "Oh, I beg your pardon!" much as if he had walked into a wrong bedroom and the spectacle of a lady brushing her teeth. But the figure was that of a middle-aged man—who might have been expected to say, "Not at all," or "Good afternoon," or "Mr. Honeybath, is it not?" or simply just, "Hallo." But from the figure there came no sound, nor did it look up or stir in its seat. Honeybath concluded that here was a fellow guest—for guests came and went—who had sought out this secluded situation for a quiet after-luncheon nap, or even for the purpose of meditation and private devotion. Thus indicting himself of idle and unseasonable behaviour, the eminent painter (whose unflawed courtesy was an unobtrusive part of his makeup) was about to withdraw as quietly as might be when he realized that something was wrong. He walked up to the seated figure, touched a hand, with his own hand made a small gesture before open and unblinking eyes, and saw that he was almost certainly in the presence of a dead man. This was a shock. There was a greater shock when he took in the expression frozen, as it were, upon the dead man's face. It could be described only as exhibiting malign glee.

So here is the finding of our corpse.

Satisfied that the man was indeed dead, Honeybath decided that it wasn't his business to interfere with the body or investigate further. He must simply hasten to apprise his host of his perturbing discovery. So he turned away to leave the library. At the door, however, he paused for a moment. There was a key in the lock on its inner side. This, on a sudden impulse, he removed to the outside, and he then locked the door behind him. He put the key in his pocket and went on his way.

Finding Grinton ought to have been easy. It was teatime, and he was likely, together at least with some of his household and guests, to be gathered in the drawing room in respectful attendance upon Dolly Grinton's Georgian silver. This very circumstance, however, made the thing awkward. To announce baldly, "There's a dead man in the library," would be a little lacking in skilled social comportment in a company possibly including several delicately nurtured gentlewomen. Honeybath saw that he must go quietly up to Grinton himself and murmur, "My dear Grinton, may I have a word with you?" This in itself might occasion slight surprise, but of course his host would at once get to his feet and leave the room with him.

The plan, however, failed to work. Even as Honeybath opened the door, Grinton appeared to have come just to the end of telling some vastly entertaining story—or at least this was the inference to be drawn from the fact that the man himself was laughing loudly, and that several people imperfectly glimpsed were politely acknowledging that general mirth was required. Honeybath, thus finding himself in something like the position of the messenger Mercadé in *Love's Labour's Lost*, bearing woeful tidings into a joyous assembly, momentarily lost his nerve and retired again, with the result that he bumped into Sir John Appleby, who was arriving rather late for tea.

"John!" Honeybath said. "There's a dead man in the library." "Are you sure?" There was nothing startled in Appleby's voice. "Sleepy places, libraries, at times. And since this one is a kind of sleeping library itself . . ."

"It isn't a joke." Honeybath, already agitated, was now annoyed as well. "A dead man, I tell you."

"Who is it?"

"I've no idea. Just a middle-aged man. I never saw him before. We must let Grinton know at once. We'd better both go in." Honeybath had seized the chance of useful reinforcement. He perhaps dimly felt that to have a retired Commissioner of Metropolitan Police at one's elbow is a welcome state of affairs when something slightly unnerving is on hand. "That's the only proper thing."

"Well, yes." Appleby wasn't in a hurry. "But if there's really a total stranger suddenly dead on the premises this Terence Grinton will create uproar at once. Tally-ho and from a view to a death will be nothing to it. I think you and I had better have a quiet look first. If you can nerve yourself to it, Charles."

"Certainly I can." Honeybath wasn't pleased at this needless challenge. It hinted a levity inappropriate to the occasion. But then John, he recalled, was one much traded in corpses. He had been dealing with them unceasingly throughout the earlier part of his professional career. In the light of this, a certain tinge of the hard-boiled in his attitude was fair enough. "Come along then," Honeybath said. "And don't imagine I've gone clean off my head."

"Certainly not." Appleby was entirely placid. "That's a most unlikely contingency. Even more unlikely than the appearance of a dead body in the library at Grinton."

They made their way in silence to the library. It was quite a step. If the squirearchal Grintons had from time to time

8

turned up men of literary or artistic inclination, so had they also produced every now and then men with an alert eye to every opportunity of augmenting the family fortune. And these money-making Grintons had commonly commemorated their success by additions—always in a contemporary taste—to the fabric of their dwelling. Grinton sprawled and proliferated in half a dozen architectural styles in a manner almost totally obscuring its original character as no more than a substantial manor house. The final result, you could feel, was much what might be achieved by a child possessed of an inordinately wide variety of "building sets" of the sophisticated modern sort. The reckless *mélange* might conceivably have produced a not unpleasing effect of fantasy. But this hadn't happened. The place was a bit of a monstrosity. Respectable guidebooks to the county said as much in decently temperate language.

The library occupied the greater part of the ground floor of a wing of moderate size and sober elegance designed by James Gibbs, an excellent architect although a suspected Jacobite, in the first quarter of the eighteenth century. Its south front remained much as Gibbs had left it, but that to the north was in part obscured by a confused huddle of domestic offices, now disused and virtually derelict, added by a Victorian Grinton with a mania for maintaining something like a small army of servants whose preservation from a scandalous idleness had required the exercise of much ingenuity on the part of the housekeeper, butler and similar important persons.

The door of the library stood at the end of, and faced down, a broad corridor. This approach Appleby and Honeybath traversed in a slightly constrained silence. The constraint was undoubtedly Appleby's creation. Much experi-

9

ence had fostered in him a sceptical stance before one or another extravagant persuasion on the part of agitated citizens. There was going to be a moment or two of mild embarrassment as the man in the library of Grinton Hall woke up.

Honeybath halted before the door and brought the key from his pocket. At this Appleby was prompted to speech.

"Good Lord, Charles! Did you lock the place up behind you?"

"Well, yes—I thought it just as well." Honeybath offered this confession rather awkwardly. "There are several children in the house, you know, and no end of women. I felt that if one of them had obeyed the same impulse as myself—an impulse of rather pointless curiosity, I fear—they might have . . ."

"Quite so. Received a terrible shock. Now go ahead."

So Honeybath unlocked the door, and the two men entered the room. The armchair was where it had been. But its occupant had vanished.

"It's not there!" This came from Honeybath as a spontaneous cry of dismay. He might have been feeling that here was a large misfortune in itself, much as if the dead man had been a valuable clock or painting.

"Well, no." Appleby looked about him at leisure. "There seems to be nothing spectacular on view for the present." He glanced at Honeybath almost with suspicion—but it was impossible to believe that so right-thinking a man had involved himself in some tasteless practical joke. "Is that the chair?"

"Definitely."

"He was slumped in it?"

"Not quite that." Honeybath was relieved at being presented with these matter-of-fact questions. "Just sitting. Or better, perhaps, perched." Here was a field in which he was, after all, an authority. "If a sitter sat like that, I'd beg him to relax." Honeybath studied the room more carefully than before. "It's like one of your sealed-room mysteries."

"One of my what?"

"Well, in thrillers, then." Honeybath felt that he had embarked on rather a foolish line of talk. "A crime or something taking place behind locked doors, so that the perpetrator couldn't seemingly have got out. Only here it's the corpse."

"Oh, that! I see." Appleby didn't sound interested. "I can't remember running across anything of the sort. But I may have. As you know, my bloodhound days are rather far behind me. But here your locked door has happened, without a doubt. Or without, at least, an immediate doubt. Your corpse has vanished through the roof, or something like that. Postmortem levitation. Or an Assumption . . ."

"Quite so." Honeybath hastened to save his friend from perpetrating a profane comparison. "There's that fireplace," he added with recovered confidence.

"So there is."

"It might be described as of baronial magnificence, wouldn't you say? Out of proportion even to this large room."

This was true. The fireplace was a huge marble affair, massively decorated with statuary and armorial bearings. Appleby obligingly inspected it with care.

"You think," he asked seriously, "the corpse may have scrambled up the chimney—like some sweep's unfortunate juvenile assistant in Victoria's darkest England?"

"Not exactly that." Honeybath felt uncomfortable in the face of this unseasonable pleasantry. "But it might have

11

been hauled up, if the flue's a straight one. Or someone may have had a rope ladder. A *silk* rope ladder. I've read that such a thing can be conveyed undetected if tightly wound round a fellow's body. Under his jacket, you know."

"Well, it might certainly be a handy thing in your sealed-room situation, Charles. But are you sure it *is* your situation?"

"There's only one door, and I locked it behind me."

"There are three windows—and very big ones, if the point's relevant. Let's look at them."

They looked at the windows.

"Not the original fenestration," Honeybath said with knowledge. "Altered in the age of plate glass. But what are those little boxes?"

"It's the age of burglar alarms, too." Appleby made a rapid inspection. "All three windows firmly secured from the inside. For the moment, your S.R.S. prospers."

"My what, John?"

"Sealed-room situation. But wait a minute! Here's a staircase—an odd little spiral one—descending to some depth below. You don't see it at first, since it's hidden in this furthest bay. I'm going down." Appleby had scarcely ceased speaking before—with remarkable agility in an elderly man—he had simply vanished beneath the floor. For a couple of minutes Honeybath heard him moving about. Then, decidedly in a dusty state, he reappeared again. "Only a very large basement," he said. "No door, just some massively barred semibasement windows. And the whole area absolutely crammed with junk. But literary and learned junk. More books, stacked up in enormous piles, higgledy-piggledy. Old trunks bulging with papers in bundles and papers in tatters. A kind of librarian's nightmare."

"How very odd."

"It's just a matter of most Grintons having been of the true Terence breed. But return to the body, Charles—in recollection, that is. Would you say you examined it at all thoroughly?"

"I can't say that I did. But I do feel I made sure the man was dead. And something about it does now come into my head—just because of your own present appearance, as a matter of fact. There was something dusty about him—and a cobweb in his hair. Do you know? I'm beginning almost to see him again." Honeybath frowned. "Something about his clothes—no, not just the dust. And about his shoes. But, no—it's gone again."

"It may come back."

"I suppose I ought to have been more observant. You see, being quite sure the man was dead, I decided to get Grinton at once."

"Quite right, but you realize where we are now. When you left the library, the probability was that you were leaving behind you a death from natural causes. Most people die that way, after all."

"Yes, of course."

"That the chap was unknown to you was perplexing, but there could be several explanations of that. When bodies immediately disappear, however, the probability shifts. Why whisk away into concealment the victim of a simple heart attack? No answer, Charles. Or none that I can see offhand. So miching mallecho seems to be at work."

Appleby was now prowling the room rather in the manner of one of the larger cats waiting to be fed in a zoo. It was a room deserving to be called handsome in every way. From the marble floor, for the most part obscured beneath dim and doubtless valuable rugs thick as autumnal leaves in Vallombrosa or similar localities, up to a deeply coffered

13

ceiling to which gilding had at some period been liberally applied, every inch of wall space was occupied by tier upon tier of books in a state of centennial slumber. More books— thousands rather than hundreds of them—were ranged in deep bays or alcoves projecting from the long north wall of the room. The total effect was oppressive, and this was enhanced by the presence of a powerful *smell*. Even well-kept books, provided they are numerous and old enough, generate this phenomenon. Confronted by all this, Honey-bath, although much distracted by the untoward situation into which he had been precipitated, spared a thought for his wonderful vision of Terence Grinton here in his hunting kit. Sitting at ease, perhaps, in that fatal chair . . .

"Learned Grintons," Appleby said. "It's a staggering thought." Appleby seemed to be judging it useful to study the books almost shelf by shelf. "The *Deipnosophists* of Athenaeus, for example. Now, just what would that be? I have a notion they were a kind of learned dining club. And here's . . . ah, yes—here it is. The dummy section, Charles. You must have seen it often enough. A childish amusement in eighteenth-century libraries. But whither, in this particular case? *Wohin der Weg?* as Faust asks Mephistopheles."

It was almost as if Appleby was excited, and old habits were overtaking him. He had done no more, of course, than locate, and pull open, a section of shelving that wasn't shelving at all, but merely a door deceptively veneered with the spines of nonexistent books. What was revealed was a further door, apparently outward-opening, and no farther off than the thickness of the library wall. To this door there was a key, but it wasn't turned in the lock.

"Now, just what lies beyond that?" Appleby was bringing a handkerchief from his pocket. "The library occupies the

14

entire breadth of the wing, so it must simply be open air. A bolt hole from learning back to nature. Books! 'tis a dull and endless strife: Come, hear the woodland linnet. Don't touch the handle, Charles. Fingerprints, you know."

Gingerly, and using the handkerchief, Appleby opened this second door upon what, according to his reckoning, ought to have been afternoon sunshine. But it wasn't.

"My dear Charles!" he exclaimed. "Just what do you make of that?"

And at this Honeybath was inspired to a little quotation dropping on his own account.

"Hellish dark," he said, "and smells of cheese."

2

THE SMELL OF CHEESE WAS UNDENIABLE. IT WAS A SMELL, indeed, of *toasted* cheese, as if somebody had lately been indulging in the humble but delectable dish facetiously known as Welsh rabbit. At half past four in the afternoon it was an unexpected smell in a dignified country house, but the explanation of this might well have lain in the fact that what Appleby and Honeybath now confronted was a seeming maze of unassuming domestic offices. If Grinton ran to anyone as archaic as a bootboy or a buttons, it was conceivable that this lowly and juvenile servitor was recruiting himself with a snack in the privacy of his own obscure quarters.

That our explorers could arrive at such speculation was due to the fact that "hellish dark" was an exaggeration on Honeybath's part. He had expected bright sunlight; what he had come upon was merely gloomy and crepuscular. There lay ahead a narrow and ill-lit corridor, with what appeared to be a considerable number of small rooms opening off it on either hand.

"But of course!" Honeybath said. "I remember now. I took a stroll round the outside of the house yesterday, and came on all this. It makes hay of poor James Gibbs's subdued Palladian design, you know. An entire little shanty town tucked into the angle between the library wing and the main building. Quarters for garden boys and stable lads by the dozen, I suppose. A monument, my dear John, to the inexpugnable philistinism—vandalism, if you like—of the English lesser landed gentry."

"It does seem a shade dismal." Appleby wondered whether Terence Grinton would care to hear himself as coming from this precise social class.

"And all entirely unused and deserted now. Nothing but an occasional rat stirring." Honeybath shook his head gloomily, but then brightened a little. "I wonder whether we could persuade the fellow to knock it all down?"

"I doubt it. And one must look ahead. The accommodation may come in handy when Grinton is turned into a dump for the delinquent young. And meanwhile we must be said to have other work on hand."

"Yes of course. The corpse." Honeybath opened a door at random and peered into a small empty room. "Come to think of it," he said, "these quarters can't be *quite* deserted. There's this smell."

"A clinging sort of smell. But it can't be lingering from eighty years back, or thereabout. Try the next room, Charles."

The next room proved to be larger, and not quite unfurnished. It contained a folding table and chair, a camp bed, several cardboard boxes, and a cooking stove fed from a small cylinder of butane gas.

"What might be called a holiday home," Appleby said. "And simple holiday fare. Observe the plate."

Honeybath observed the plate. It stood on the folding table, and on it lay a knife and fork and a substantial slice of

17

toasted cheese. There was also a glass of water, and a small medicine bottle, unlabelled, and half full of pills.

"I suppose they're really there?" Appleby asked with an effect of mild humour. "We're not just dreaming something up?"

"They're there, all right." As if to reassure himself of this, Honeybath advanced and poked the plate with a cautious finger. "Cold," he said.

"Which at least suggests that a solitary feast wasn't interrupted no more than five minutes ago. Can we gather anything else from this small spectacle?"

"Well, half the feast is unconsumed. Perhaps the feaster's eye was bigger than his belly. Or his digestion wasn't too good."

"The pills might suggest that."

"Yes—but perhaps it was something quite different. Perhaps he was suddenly alerted or alarmed."

"Right enough, Charles. But what about a third possibility? Toasted cheese is rather a perfunctory and uninteresting dish. The mind of this lurking character is elsewhere. Some notion suddenly starts up in his mind so commandingly that he must follow it at once. He shoves his plate aside, hurries back to the library—and never again leaves it alive. So the cheese is important, as you can see."

"Important?" It was with a touch of irritation that Honeybath repeated the word. "For heaven's sake, John, don't start talking to me in Sherlock Holmes riddles. This whole business has upset me very much. It's quite some time since I stumbled on a dead body."

"Sorry—and of course it's all thoroughly conjectural. The plate may very well have been cold from the first. But I do somehow like the idea of his jumping up half way through his meal, whether because he was somehow alerted to your

18

entering the library and finding the corpse, or because some exciting notion had suddenly got hold of him."

"It may be a woman, not a man."

"There's a statistical improbability there. The male sex has the stronger predilection for toasted cheese. Females eat poached eggs."

Charles Honeybath compressed his lips. He rather envied his friend this ruthless chauvinism. But he considered it indecorous, all the same.

"John," he asked, "I take it you believe us to be in the presence of a crime?"

"It's a working hypothesis. We might be more confident about it if you'd thought to take a better look at that dead man."

"Yes, of course. I see that." Honeybath paused, and it turned out to be in search of a small levity of his own. "I'll try harder next time." He paused again, not being at all happy with this. "There's one thing I did notice," he said. "It was the expression on the dead man's face. I thought of it as malign glee. Really that. A malicious grin, as if he was pleased about something, or enjoying a nasty joke."

"Rictus," Appleby said—but with more of perplexity than conviction. "A big gape often remarked in what you might call sudden corpses. It used to be noticed when they'd hanged people."

Honeybath felt that he could have done without this information. He also felt increasingly bewildered, and now expressed the fact.

"I can't make head or tail of it," he said.

"I wouldn't say that. The head and tail are there, all right—although I admit that, even metaphorically speaking, the body is still to seek. As you are a perfectly reliable witness, my dear Charles, we have this: there in the library

19

was a dead man; you came upon it, and at once proceeded, very properly, to tell our host; you left the library for that purpose, locking the door behind you; some person or persons, with the alternative means of ingress and egress we have discovered, almost at once took alarm and removed the body, the whereabouts of which are now unknown to us. Right?"

"Certainly."

"This room seems to have been in the more or less temporary occupation of a single person. A single bed, and what you might term catering for one—and pills for one—make that point clear. It doesn't follow that only one person was involved in the total operation—whatever the total operation may have been. Metaphorically again, it's the total operation—the teleological aspect of the thing, so to speak—that is the missing body. The why and wherefore entirely elude us at the moment. Right again?"

"Yes." Honeybath, although a little distrustful of the philosophical embellishment given to this serious of propositions, could only agree. "Do we now hunt around further on our own, or do we call in assistance first?"

"An immediate alarm, and sending for the police and so forth, would be the proper thing. But we can give ourselves another ten minutes or so of impropriety. Fossick around this odd setup a little."

"There may be a lurking miscreant—or miscreants." Honeybath is not to be charged with offering this observation apprehensively. He was necessarily an imaginative man, or he wouldn't have succeeded as a fashionable portrait painter. But although he could conjure up risks and horrors with some facility, he was by nature a courageous person. Nevertheless, he thought to ask a question.

"John, are you armed?"

"*Armed?*"

"Carrying a gun, or something of the sort."

"Good lord!" Appleby refrained from laughter. "Guns and sealed rooms go together, my dear chap. Their natural home is in your storybooks. And now we'll take a look at the other rooms in this abandoned Grinton slum."

They looked at half a dozen rooms. The disagreeable accredtions to the library's north front proved to be, after all, not strikingly extensive. Here and there were a few sticks of abandoned furniture, but apart from these the rooms harboured nothing except dust and cobweb.

"Not even a bat, owl, or temple-haunting martlet," Appleby said. "Let's find our way into the open air. The approach to these *aedes liberae* may be instructive."

"You're being devilish learned," Honeybath said—peevishly but not unreasonably.

"It happens with detectives, in a sporadic way. Your pal Sherlock Holmes, for instance. On one page his knowledge of literature is pronounced to be *nil*. On another you find him quoting Goethe or Flaubert in the original."

"Bother Sherlock Holmes! And he's *not* my pal. It's years since . . ." Honeybath fell silent, aware of something childish in his attitude. And he realized that his friend (like some further Holmeses, come to think of it) was given to talking nonsense while he thought hard. "Here's the outside door, John. And it's not locked. There's not even a key."

They emerged into a space having the character of a small stable yard. It had a forlorn air, and it was clear that nothing much happened in it. An abandoned piece of agricultural machinery stood in a corner, and in another was what appeared to be a snowplough. There was an empty shed which might have housed a car or small van.

"There's a kind of cart track straight ahead," Appleby said.

"Yes, I noticed it yesterday. I think it joins a secondary drive: not the grand one through the park, but a humble one leading by a short route to the village and the church. The equivalent of the suburban tradesmen's entrance, one may say."

"No doubt. But Charles, here's the important thing. Some fairly recent Grinton has had the grace to be ashamed of this mess, and has managed that enormous hedge. Positively Italian, isn't it? And in very good trim."

"Your important point being that it entirely screens all this from the main building?"

"Just that—or almost that. If one walked straight across this yard one might be overseen from the top windows. But not if one skirted it on the house side. I believe it would even be possible to bring in a car or van. Risky, of course. But it could be done."

"Particularly at night."

"Particularly at night." Appleby nodded gravely, as if in tribute to this sagacious remark. "And, of course, if there was no moon."

"But people like the Grintons go in for dogs in a big way. Indeed, I believe Grinton receives superannuated foxhounds within his domestic circle. I've already been sniffed at by several such creatures. And the dogs might bark."

"Or not bark, Charles. That is the really significant thing. The sedge is withered from the lake, and no dogs woof."

With this peculiarly extravagant perversion of Keats and Conan Doyle, Appleby led the way back to the library.

But then—rather to Honeybath's surprise—he lingered

there. It might almost have been said that the retired Commissioner lingered there wistfully. And, as if aware of betraying this oddity of feeling, he explained himself.

"It's the police, all right," he said. "A simple dead body can be coped with, at least in the first instance, by the family doctor. He arrives with his little black bag, pronounces life to be extinct, and then conceivably has to wonder whether establishing the cause of death requires a p-m. An autopsy, as the jargon has it nowadays. But, Charles, a *missing* dead body is quite another matter. You report it to your local police station; uniformed men turn up in a miraculous ten minutes; as soon as they're satisfied that the affair isn't nonsense they get on the blower; and the plainclothes chaps from their detective branch are likely to be with you ten minutes after that again. And all this in the sleepiest part of the country you care to choose. The Fire Brigade just isn't in it. The speed of the operation can be very disconcerting."

"I suppose that must be so." Honeybath looked doubtfully at his friend.

"I myself shall be in danger of becoming irritated. They won't let me in, you know. Not into this library again. It would be dead against all policemanly etiquette. Not like all those fairy tales you have in your head, with the thickheaded Inspector hurrying forward and crying out 'Thank God you're here, sir.'"

"John, don't be idiotic. I have no such . . ."

"But it's you, Charles, that I'm thinking of." Appleby pressed on—heedlessly and handsomely. "You have such an extraordinary yarn to tell them, you see. A vanishing corpse! They'll be conscientiously bound to assume that you're either off your head or having them on. Probably the latter. They have a kind of folklore about houses like this

23

and their inhabitants. Wild carouses and crazy wagers. *A* bets *B* he can persuade *C* to plunge the telephone into a bucket of water. That kind of thing. So this vanishing corpse *is* nonsense, they'll tell each other, and agree that their uniformed colleagues were right thickies to suppose anything else. And they'll interrogate you on that basis. Three or four of them, all gathered round."

"John, I really think this kind of fun . . ."

"I'm sorry." Appleby was perhaps genuinely abashed. "But I'm serious, in a way. You will find the whole routine trying, I'm afraid. But others may find it more trying still. There's a fair-sized party at Grinton this weekend. I've no reason to suppose there's much in the way of dubious goings-on. But people don't like having their movements inquired into in an *alibi*-seeking way. Of course it mayn't come to all that. But it very well may."

"Aren't you being a bit portentous, my dear chap?" Honeybath was rallying. "My own story is rather macabre but quite simple, and I shan't in the least mind being questioned by your policemen."

"Good. But, by the way, don't start offering them conjectures."

"Conjectures?"

"Well, take this. Remember our brief exchange about the pose or posture of the body? Slumped or perched? That sort of thing. 'If a sitter sat like that, I'd beg him to relax.' I think you said that to me. Repeat it to a competent detective officer, and he'll be on to something at once. *Rigor mortis*. Did the appearance of the body, he'll ask, suggest that well-known postmortem condition to you? Did you by any chance *feel* a joint or limb? Well, it's an important point, of course, in attempting to determine the time of death. But I imagine it was just not in your head—and

24

you'll do no good cudgelling it for what was never there, or starting to say things of the 'I rather think' variety. Leave the other fellow to do the rather thinking."

"I'll take your advice, John." Honeybath saw that, behind a smoke screen of badinage, Appleby was genuinely concerned over the harassment he was bound to endure. "Will there be an inquest, do you suppose? Can a coroner, I mean, sit on a body that isn't there?"

"Certainly not in such circumstances as we have here now. I'm bound to say a spot or two of blood would be useful."

"A spot or two of blood?" For a moment, Honeybath was both horrified and bewildered.

"Just that. Let's have a good look at that chair, and at the rugs round about. Not that there aren't plenty of ways of killing a man without shedding gore."

Appleby carried out this investigation while Honeybath stood by. The effort was apparently unrewarding.

"Nothing doing," Appleby said. "Although, mark you, it's astonishing what the forensic chaps can conjure up out of what seems to be empty air."

"You mean, the idea that I'm of a disordered mind. . . ?"

"No, no—I've told you already. They won't assert that you've eaten of the insane root that takes the reason prisoner. But remember that it has proved, after all, not to have been a sealed room that you left behind you when you turned that key in the door. Suppose it *was* only a slumbering student that you came upon, and suppose he knew about that concealed exit. He had only to wake up and take himself off."

"A student, did you say?" Not surprisingly, Honeybath was distinctly at a loss.

"Or scholar. Conceivably quite a ripe scholar. A Regius

Professor from one of our ancient universities, or somebody like that. Sufficiently distinguished to lend tone to
this whole affair."

"John, I do appeal to you . . ."

"I'm not just being funny, Charles. I'm putting forward a
perfectly tenable hypothesis. And it explains, doesn't it,
even the toasted cheese?"

Honeybath pulled himself together. He wasn't dull, and
he now vindicated the fact.

"You mean," he asked, "that somebody has been pursu-
ing a course of clandestine research in this library—and so
much at leisure as to have fixed himself up sleeping quarters and culinary arrangements next door?"

"Just that. The academic term for it is pernoctation. The
chap pernoctates. Remains in residence night and day."

"You really believe I may have been mistaken . . ."

"I don't really believe anything of the kind." Appleby
was a shade impatient. "What I do believe is that you entered this library and found a dead man. Even so, a certain
amount of what I've just said may apply. The waking-up
and making-off theory isn't mine. It's just something that
may occur to somebody else."

"But why ever should anybody be researching here in
such a crazily covert fashion?"

"Because of the peculiar disposition of our host. Judith
has told me quite a lot about your prospective sitter. Terence Grinton actively dislikes his library, associating it with
what he regards as loopy egghead Grintons who have
turned up from time to time. It's not an altogether uncommon thing. There have been Coleridges, for instance,
who took a thoroughly dark view of Sam as the family's
black sheep. And would even have liked to shoo enquiring

scholars from the door. Can't you imagine our Terence roaring at such people?"

"Yes, I can." Honeybath now acknowledged this with candour. "But if the man *was* dead, he can't have come to life again and simply walked out of the place. He must have been smuggled out."

"Quite so. And I don't suggest that we have really got all that far. Merely penetrated to one conceivable tip of a mystery. However, let's be off. Just lock the door beyond those fake books, Charles, remembering again not to touch the handle. And we'll lock the main door behind us, just as you did before."

A couple of minutes later, the two men walked in sober silence away from the library.

3

IT WAS HONEYBATH, APPLEBY INSISTED, WHO MUST TELL
Terence Grinton what had happened. He had made an
abortive attempt to do so already, and it was in his court
that the ball still bounced. To be led by the hand, so to
speak, into his host's presence, and there to stand silent
while his disturbing discovery was recounted by a third
person, would be altogether undignified. That Appleby
happened to be a retired policeman, and so more
habituated to talking about corpses, was neither here nor
there.

Appleby didn't precisely articulate these remarks, but he
conveyed the sense of them, all the same. So thus it had to
be. Honeybath felt the occasion to be awkward, but didn't
really take much account of the fact. The one thing not
doubtful about the whole affair was its gravity. Embarrass-
ments, therefore, didn't much matter.

They found that Grinton and his wife were now alone in
the drawing room, except for the presence of a guest called
Hillam. Hillam, a middle-aged man of no considerable
presence whether physical or otherwise, was understood to
be a Curator of something somewhere, and a recent acqui-

sition to Dolly Grinton's circle of acquaintance. Nobody had been paying much attention to him, and nobody paid any attention to him now.

"Grinton," Honeybath said firmly, "I am afraid I have something most unpleasant to tell you about. Less than an hour ago, I went into your library . . ."

"The devil you did!" Grinton said. He didn't say this rudely, but he did say it violently, and his achieving this combination of effects was disconcerting. Mrs. Grinton was cheerfully amused—which was frequently her line.

"I hope it wasn't intrusive," Honeybath said, thus momentarily shying away from his proper business. "As a matter of fact, I had the thought that it might provide not a bad setting for our portrait."

"God bless my soul!" Grinton was receiving this information as a joke—a joke perhaps in rather poor taste, but which it was incumbent on a host to take in good part. "The portrait? My dear chap!"

"I found a dead man there."

"You found a *dead* man!" Grinton allowed himself to be checked for a second before this surprising information—just as he might have been on recollecting that beyond rather a high hedge lay a distinctly wide and deep ditch. "The library is crammed with dead men. Acres of them on every wall. Dead as doornails, but all still thinking themselves entitled to be taken down and listened to. Go on."

Honeybath found some difficulty in going on. Here was something he had to paint, and hadn't yet taken the measure of: a rip-roaring roast-beef-and-ale kind of philistine who yet possessed certain odd qualities of mind.

"He was simply sitting in a chair in the middle of the room," Honeybath managed to articulate. "He was somebody I'd certainly never seen before."

"Whether alive or dead—eh?" Almost predictably, Grinton judged this question deserving of brief but loud mirth. "Appleby, were you in on this artistic reconnaissance?"

"No, I was not. But I've been in the library with Honeybath again since."

"And viewed the body?"

"No. The body has now disappeared."

"Disappeared!" It was as if here at last was something about which a just indignation must be expressed. "A dead body has *disappeared* from my library? It's monstrous! I'll send for the police. Dolly, get on the telephone and tell them we've all gone mad. Insist on speaking to a man called Denver. A capable chap. Dealt very well with those demonstrators who tried to bugger up the meet at Starveacre Cross. Beg pardon, my dear." This apology for improper language was addressed to his wife. "Disappeared, my arse!" he then added as an afterthought.

"Ought you really to do that?" Unexpectedly, the little man called Hillam intervened with this, laying down a copy of *Country Life* at which he had been glancing as he did so. "Hadn't we better let Mr. Honeybath sleep it off first?"

This extremely offensive remark brought Mrs. Grinton into action.

"Sir John," she said, "is the best person to decide about that. John, ought we to get the police at once?"

"Certainly."

"There really can't be—well, some sort of mistake?"

"No."

"It does sound peculiar."

"It *is* peculiar, Dolly. And so are certain other circumstances for which I can vouch."

"Perhaps we ought to have another look in the library ourselves, John?"

"The police ought to be the first people to go in there

30

now. And somewhere else, as well. There really is a mystery to clear up, and a dead man really does figure in it. Just conceivably, no major crime is involved. I can't yet say whether that's my own conjecture."

"Denver, is it?" Mrs. Grinton said, and rose and left the room.

Among the four men, left to themselves, there was a brief silence which was broken by Hillam.

"I hope you didn't mind my little joke," Hillam said.

Honeybath, feeling that this form of words need not be construed as an apology, said nothing. Grinton looked uncomfortable—indeed, oddly ill at ease. Conceivably he was thinking that Hillam must be all right, since Dolly had brought him along, but that he wasn't quite one's own sort, all the same. Honeybath, on the other hand, was at least out of the right stable, although daubing paint on to canvas was an odd manner of life. About Appleby he wasn't at all sure. He had married one of those Ravens, who had been a crazy crowd for ages, and before that people had probably never heard of him. He had drive—Grinton had great respect for drive provided it didn't take a man too close to the heels of the pack—and had been very high up in whatever he had been high up in. This was the sum total of Terence Grinton's knowledge about Appleby. He was a man of limited curiosities.

Honeybath was trying to remember something about the opprobrious Hillam. He had never met him before, and his name was unfamiliar. Hallam Hillam—an infelicitous combination, because awkward on the tongue. Might he be some kind of art boffin? The Courtauld? The Tate? The Victoria and Albert? More probably some minor provincial place.

Appleby was telling himself not to start asking questions.

He had no personal interest in any of the people at Grinton. He was here at all only because Judith had a notion that one ought "occasionally to move among" one's quite remote connections. No doubt he had taken on the doctrine when, long ago, he had taken on the wife—and he had to admit that it had yielded interest and amusement from time to time. But a large social circle was something which neither his earliest years nor his later intellectual habit had taught him to rejoice in. Familiarity with a wide diversity of human types no doubt broadened the mind, but his professional career had provided him with quite enough of that. Pottering around the old home—really Judith's old home—and listening to his clever children's odd modish persuasions and reading this and that in order to mitigate his immense ignorance in various fields of knowledge: these were the proper employments for an aging man. Certainly not going fishing and inquiring over casually encountered petty mystifications.

"Grinton," he suddenly heard himself saying, "does your library contain much, or anything, of major interest or high value?"

"My dear chap!"

Terence Grinton seemed so astonished by this weird question—behaviour, indeed—on the part of his guest that he forgot either to roar with laughter or to bristle with indignation.

"Ask me another," he said. "People have turned up from time to time wanting to poke about in it for one crackpot reason or another. It's because of something running in my family, you know. Like drink or lunacy or chasing ceaselessly after wenches. Respectable in its own way, no doubt, among people of the appropriate sort. Not that such cattle don't turn out pretty shady if you take a hard look at them.

Beaks and dons and poets and every kind of scribbler. Communists to a man." Grinton made a brief pause in this extraordinary speech. "And they're not even always after the bloody books. Heads full of letters and diaries and heaven knows what scribblings that they imagine the place must be stuffing with. Damned impertinence. Only a few months ago there was an unnatural woman—heaven knows from where—who said she was writing a book about Ambrose Grinton, a dissolute chap who went messing around back in the Middle Ages among artists and their doxies— beg pardon, Honeybath—and collected rubbish from their wastepaper baskets. I wasn't unfriendly. I ever asked her if she ever rode to hounds, and offered to mount her for a good run or two."

"But she didn't want to be mounted?" This came from Hillam, who had appeared to be absorbed in *Country Life* again. "Or not by you?"

For a moment it looked as if this outrageous equivoque was going to be greeted with a roar of laughter. But then Grinton pulled himself up.

"She was at least a lady," he said stiffly. "So I don't follow you." He paused for a moment. "*Sir*," he added ominously.

Thus to apostrophize a guest in one's own house was pretty stiff, and Honeybath hastened to intervene— although it had to be with the first thing that came into his head.

"Having things of high value around," he said, "can create a great deal of bother with one's insurance people. I've often heard about that from owners of valuable pictures. They're told they must take all sorts of devilishly expensive precautions before they can get cover. And Appleby and I noticed you had pretty effective-looking burglar alarms fitted to the library windows."

"Is that so? That must be Dolly. It's Dolly who sees to that sort of thing."

Honeybath had been about to add—as a mere item of general interest—that the exercise had appeared to miss out on the dummy bookshelves in the library. But as this omission might now appear to reflect on Grinton's wife, he held his peace. Appleby, however, pursued the subject. (So much for his resolve to refrain from fishing.)

"Family papers make another problem," he said. "A man like yourself, Grinton, is liable to have quite a lot of them—perhaps stretching over centuries. Indeed, you've hinted something of the sort. Not of legal significance, or even of much historical importance. But precious in terms of what may be called ancestral feeling and piety. It's hard to get a cash value set on such an archive, since no marketplace exists for it. Is there anything of that sort in the library?"

"The kennel books." Grinton produced this with sudden decision and interest. "In fact the entire records of the Nether Barset since it was first recognizably a hunt. My father had a fellow working on the stuff for nearly a year, and I myself had the results bound up in decently tooled morocco. About a dozen volumes, I'd say—and no doubt still there. Not that I've made a recce in the bloody morgue for a good many years."

This sudden proclamation of Terence Grinton's notorious and eccentric attitude to his library brought the conversation to a halt. Honeybath thought of asking, "All that shifting of county boundaries has pretty well done away with Barsetshire, hasn't it?" But as this would sound like the feeblest and most irrelevant of curiosities, he contented himself with walking over to a window and surveying the February scene. And a moment later Dolly Grinton returned to the room.

"Your reliable Denver is on his way," she said cheerfully to her husband. "The copper on the telephone said Inspector Denver. Does one address him as that, or just as Mr. Denver?"

"Definitely as Mr. Denver." Appleby was impressed by this care for the forms in face of what was, after all, a trying situation. "If I were speaking to him tête-à-tête, and didn't know him, I'd probably just say 'Inspector.' But in a general way 'Mr. Denver' will be right." Appleby offered this not very important information rather absently. He was wondering whether competence in dealing with a mob of bearded persons intent on creating nasty smells to confuse a pack of foxhounds would effectively exercise itself in face of the present conundrum. Whether the conundrum ought to be described as also having a really nasty smell was yet to appear.

"I've told Burrow to show Mr. Denver straight in here," Dolly Grinton said. Burrow as the Grintons' butler. "Ought I to have said the library?"

"No, not the library." Appleby, although resolved to give nobody any instructions about anything, was obliged to say this. "As a matter of fact, Charles and I locked it up behind us. It seemed the proper thing. Grinton, here's the key."

Grinton accepted the key almost with reluctance. It symbolized, Appleby reflected, his proprietorship of something of which he strongly disapproved.

"The gentleman from the police."

Burrow thus exercised his own judgement as to what was appropriate in this matter of nomenclature as he ushered Denver into the drawing room. Denver, it appeared, had come out to Grinton on his own. Decidedly he wasn't a fussy or self-important man. His concern might have been merely a routine matter involving some hitch or inadvertence over a gun licence. He did, however, produce a large notebook as an essential concomitant of whatever proceedings were in view.

"If I might just make a note or two," he said, "on the household. Quite a large household, I expect, so it will be convenient."

"You mean who's at Grinton now?" The proprietor of Grinton seemed to feel that this put the matter more plainly. "My wife and myself, as you can see. My daughter, Magda, and her husband and two kids. They're all out after rabbits."

"Rabbits," Denver said, with a disconcerting appearance of actually having written down this word. "Yes?"

"Half a dozen guests. Or is it eight? My wife will know. I suppose she also knows something about the gentleman in the corner there. Name of Hillam, I believe." Grinton contrived this outrage without any effect of insolence. "And this is Mr. Charles Honeybath, who says he . . . found the body. Mr. Honeybath is a painter."

"Artist, or interior decorator?"

"Don't be a fool, Denver. Mr. Honeybath is a most distinguished artist. Otherwise he wouldn't be here."

"Distinguished," Denver said—without any appearance of displeasure. "A friend of long standing, I take it?"

"Nothing of the kind." Grinton perhaps felt that this was a slightly unbecoming expression. "But an old friend of Sir John and Lady Appleby. This is Sir John. Lady Appleby has gone for a walk."

"Sir John and Lady Appleby," Denver repeated as he wrote—and in an inexpressive fashion that pleased Appleby very much. "And who else? I needn't have the servants, just at the moment, Mr. Grinton."

Grinton gave the required names, accompanying several of them with more or less gratuitous comments. Denver wrote them all down, and then closed his notebook. He did this with an air of feeling that to keep it open would be discourteous during the next phase of the enquiry.

"Mr. Honeybath," he said. "You appear to have had a most upsetting experience. Nobody expects to come on a body when he goes to find a book in a library."

"I didn't go to find a book." Honeybath judged that this misconception must be removed at once. "I just went to look at the place. I hadn't been in it before."

"Ah! Quite natural, of course. And you mustn't let my questions worry you."

"I have no such disposition, Mr. Denver." Honeybath said this a trifle disingenuously. Worry was of course the precise word for the whole thing. "So go ahead."

Denver went ahead, and the story—the unlikely story—unfolded. Denver took it in his stride, and didn't again apply himself to the notebook.

"And now I'd better have a look," he said when it was concluded. "At the library, I mean. With your permission, sir."

Grinton grunted acquiescence in so decidedly ungracious a manner that any common policeman might have become suspicious at once. But the gracelessness—it was to be presumed—was a matter of habit and not of guilt on Grinton's part.

"Anybody in there now?" Denver asked.

"We locked it up," Appleby said, and immediately felt that he ought to have left this reply to Honeybath. Appleby's line was absolute invisibility until he was, so to speak, unmasked. It had sounded as if Inspector Denver had no recollection of Scotland Yard as once having harboured a Sir John Appleby. It wasn't likely. But it was a nice thought.

"Then we'll go along." Denver took the initiative in moving towards the door of the drawing room—thereby offering a delicate indication that he was in control of the proceedings. "But not too many of us, since we don't want a great deal of moving about in the place. It's possible that I may have to bring in men to look for fingerprints, and that sort of thing. Mr. Honeybath, of course, as well as yourself, Mr. Grinton. And perhaps you'll be good enough to come with us as well, Sir James."

"John," Appleby said.

"I beg your pardon. Sir John." Denver was at his most wooden. "And, of course, we must have a look at this place in which it seems that somebody has been putting up for the night. It's an odd one, that. If I were sceptical before improbabilities—which isn't, you know, a detective officer's business: far from it—I think I'd be sceptical there. After you, sir."

Grinton produced another grunt, and the four men left the room.

The appearance of the library had changed a little. This was because the direct late-afternoon sunlight was now only slanting through the three tall south windows, and creating shadows where there had been none before. There was also a fine dust dancing and eddying in its beams, as if stirred into motion by the mere opening of the door. It would be quite something, Honeybath told himself, to snare just that on a canvas. The floor was interesting, too. He noticed for the first time that the marble, where not concealed in a rather stupid way by the multicoloured rugs, was of a cold silver-grey heavily streaked with trailing strands of dark green. The effect, particularly in certain bays created by the additional book stacks jutting out into the room, was cavernous and almost subaquatic. *The superannuations of sunk realms* . . . He wondered where the quotation came from.

"Is that the chair?" Denver asked.

It had been Appleby's first question too. Honeybath looked at the chair, and for the first time saw the question's prompting occasion.

"Yes, it is."

"You didn't by any chance move it, Mr. Honeybath?"

"Most certainly not."

"It's a little oddly placed, isn't it? Planted there, and directly facing the door. Not really related to what you might call the general lie of the room. Everything else *is* related, somehow, to whatever's round about it. To rather a formal and unused effect, in a way."

"The place *is* unused." Its owner said this with a certain morose satisfaction. "We're not bookish at Grinton. I sometimes call the library the great family white elephant." Grinton, who hadn't roared with laughter for some time, roared with laughter now. Then he checked himself. "Beg pardon," he said. "Dead man and all that."

"But there isn't a dead man." Denver betrayed mild exasperation as he said this. "But of course there was one," he added hastily. "In that chair. Just what do you make of it, sir?"

This appeal, being addressed abruptly to Appleby, was disconcerting. But there was no point in affecting to be obtuse.

"When Mr. Honeybath first spoke to me about it," Appleby said, "he made a remark about a sitter posed for a portrait. It was merely something running in his head, since it's to paint a portrait that he's at Grinton now. But it suggested something to me: a body set in that chair and pointing just that way. It suggested a deliberate extravagance—a flamboyance, say, or a very grisly joke. Somebody was to come into this library and receive a nasty shock. It's a tenuous notion. But it came to me."

"It might come to anybody," Denver said—perhaps not wholly felicitously. "But it's worth thinking about. Mr. Grinton, who would be likely to come into this room and have that happen to him?"

"Her," Grinton said. "Almost certainly, her. One of the maids comes in once a week—on what day I don't know, although my wife probably does. Flicks around with one of those feather things."

"I see." Denver was silent for a moment, perhaps perpending the absurdity of such a pitiful onslaught on thousands of books. "But occasion might be found to get somebody else to come in? An interested party—to put it that way—might have thought to contrive that you yourself should come in and be surprised by the thing?"

"Most unlikely." Grinton gave this reply with a robust confidence. "And this is all rubbish, anyway. What's the use of talking about a dead body when there isn't one?"

Denver made no reply to such confused logic. Much as Appleby had done before him, he was studying the chair with minute attention. He then applied the same technique to the library at large, so that his companions might have begun to feel that they were all going to be there till dinner time. But quite soon he gave it up.

"There's absolutely nothing," he said. "It's all as normal

and innocent as may be. Of course we can bring people in, you know, whose line is to produce marvels. They'll analyse the dust—of which there's enough, I must say—and they'll analyse the lord knows what. They'll tell you how many different people, if any, have been in this room over the past week. Tell you their sex, for that matter, and perhaps the colour of their hair. But it takes time. And I won't say what I think it leads to."

Appleby liked this, perhaps as himself having similar phases of bafflement stacked up pretty abundantly in his past. And the momentary sense of fellow feeling prompted him to break that resolve to keep almost entirely mum.

"At least," he said, "we can now go next door. Architecturally speaking, it's to move from the sublime to the ridiculous. There's a little warren of small domestic offices—grotesquely opening, as I've told you, from behind an imposing stack of bogus seventeenth-century theology, if I remember aright. But at least there's something on view. Even toasted cheese is better than nothing."

"Marginally, perhaps." Slight gloom appeared to be possessing Denver.

"Incidentally, I suppose the state of those doors and keys is important." Appleby produced this conjecture with splendid vagueness. "But Mr. Honeybath will be clearerheaded about that than I am."

This was a bit steep—or at least Honeybath thought so. But he did his best.

"Sir John and I," he said, "found a door behind the false one unlocked but with a key in it. A further door, giving on a yard outside, was unlocked and without a key. That's perhaps a little surprising. And those offices must be connected in some further way, I imagine, with the main building. We didn't investigate that. I think it was unnecessary because, before going to look for Mr. Grinton, we locked both these entrances to the library itself. But one sees that the body may have been removed—when it was removed during my very brief absence—in one of two ways: either into the yard and then whisked away in a conveyance, or back into the house itself through the far end of these offices. The latter course would surely have been extremely hazardous, and is therefore much the less probable."

As brief exposition, Appleby thought rather well of this. He thought rather less well of himself, since he ought to have checked up on that presumed further entrance from the offices to the main building. The point was not perhaps other than a merely academic one, since Honeybath was undoubtedly right about the vast unlikelihood of the body's having simply been smuggled into another part of the house. Still, he wasn't what he once had been, Appleby thought. So he became a shade gloomy too.

They passed through the bogus door, unlocked the proper door beyond it, and passed through that. Denver made a pause in the corridor thus revealed.

"The squatter," he said. "Have I got this clear? We're going to come on evidence of a person or persons actually living in a clandestine way on the premises? It's a new one to me, I must say."

"Nevertheless, that's it." Appleby threw open a door. "Here's the first room—totally empty, as you see. And here's what you may call the lodging house." He threw open the door of the second room.

But the second room was now totally empty too.

4

NATURALLY ENOUGH, APPLEBY WASN'T PLEASED. PROB-
ably Honeybath wasn't pleased either, but with Honeybath
nothing in the nature of professional prestige was involved.
Appleby felt that he had put something almost approaching
theatricality into ushering his provincial colleague into the
presence of a camp bed, a cooking stove and whatever, and
that there was something awkward in the fact that the designed effect had decidedly not come off.

But if anybody actually showed embarrassment it was
Detective Inspector Denver. Whether Denver really knew
who Appleby was, or was as unknowing as he appeared to
be, he was in the presence of two guests at Grinton who
were both obviously of some standing in the world, and
who had somehow involved themselves in what—at least at
a first glance—looked like an episode of obscure farce.

Three of the four men, then, were uncomfortably silent
for several moments. Not so Terence Grinton. If anything
had its funny side, it was in Grinton's nature to seize upon
it with acclaim. So Grinton now produced that roar. Here
was the funniest thing that had happened for a long time.
One mare's nest, he was apparently feeling, had riotously
succeeded upon another.

It may be presumed that Denver, being a clear-headed man, was at once able to distinguish between one episode and the other. Honeybath and Appleby had entered this room together, and what they had found in it they had reported upon without any divergence of statement between them. It was true that one did occasionally come upon two—or even more—perfectly respectable witnesses swearing to an identical experience that in the issue had proved radically without status as objective fact. Of this there usually turned out to be now one explanation and now another. Human minds were uncommonly rum, and could run even to what psychologists called collective hallucination. Denver had more than once stood by and witnessed even judges of the High Court baffled by such situations. Denver, however, as a reasonable man, could come to only one conclusion here. Barring something in the nature of an irresponsible prank or scandalous wager—in which he didn't for a moment believe—these two gentlemen had seen exactly what they said they saw. And this meant that in the space of what could be reckoned as well under an hour a person or persons unknown had entered this room and done a thorough clear-up. This had been at least at appreciable risk of detection, since the yard—and presumably a vehicle in the yard—might well have been observed: this even taking account of the considerable seclusion of the entire area. Either, therefore, there had been something deadly serious about the exploit, or it exemplified the same sort of freakish behaviour as had been at work in the deliberate perching (as it could be read to be) of that body in the adjacent library.

But had there *been* a body? Denver was bound to have been asking himself this. Honeybath's story had a quite different standing from the joint story of Honeybath and

Appleby. Honeybath was an artist, and therefore more or less by definition a fanciful and unreliable person. It was of course improbable that he went in for hallucinations in a big way. But he might well have come upon a man deeply asleep, and have jumped to the conclusion—this on the score of some mild temperamental quirk of his own—that it was a dead man he was looking at. And almost immediately upon his quitting the library the man might have woken up, and taken through the bogus door the shortest route to a reviving toddle in open air.

Hither and thither dividing the swift mind, therefore, Inspector Denver must be thus thought of as he glanced round the unrewarding vacancy before him.

"There isn't much to go on," he then said.

Appleby wasn't so sure. His own first conjecture offered at least a small niche or crevice in the blank wall the Grinton affair presented as a whole. One hears of industrial espionage—and often of a highly ingenious and even *outré* sort. So why not learned or academic espionage? The Grinton library was an absolutely unknown quantity. A lot of it would be rubbish or near rubbish, of no more value than the sham volumes of outmoded theology on the concealed door. As much again, or more, must consist of books which time and comparative rarity had made worth, in the aggregate, a good deal of money. But nothing of this kind was likely to be so important, or so impossible of access elsewhere, as to produce the extraordinary state of affairs which Appleby believed himself to have stumbled on. Only highly significant manuscript material would fill the bill. But, if found, why not simply make off with it? Perhaps there was a moral, conceivably also a legal, distinction be-tween filching something and simply studying or copying it even in a clandestine and trespassing way on the spot. *But perhaps it had to be searched for.* Nothing was more likely than that, catalogue-wise, the Grinton library and its cellarage were a chaos.

All this made sense in a way. But it didn't quite make sense of a dead body. That seemed to belong with another order of activity. And in all this there was a good deal of food for thought.

Was there anyone at Grinton who was likely really to know about the library? Terence Grinton himself was an obvious write-off from the start. He knew about the kennel books, and he believed that a certain forbear called Ambrose Grinton, who was most unlikely to have flourished more than two or three centuries ago, belonged "back in the middle ages." Dolly Grinton was clearly a more sophisticated person, with some education and a good deal of intelligence. But Dolly's taste in literature and the arts in general had already made itself known to Appleby as of a modish sort, and it was likely that she owned only a sketchy knowledge of the history of the family into which she had married. She was also rather Frenchified, and liked talking about Robbe-Grillet, Nathalie Sarraute, *la nouvelle vague,* and topics of that kind: no doubt noteworthy in themselves but having little to do with English squirarchal life. Appleby had noticed, however, that Judith, who kept up a little with that sort of passing show, had been getting on very well with Dolly. If anything that could be classified as mere family gossip looked like being relevant to the present mystery it could possibly be coaxed into light by this route.

Was there anyone else? The Grintons' daughter and son-in-law, Magda and Giles Tancock, together with their two children and a nurse, were staying at Grinton for a week.

46

Terence Grinton had early described Tancock to Appleby as a "glorified auctioneer," but had not been specific as to just where the glorification lay. Perhaps he shouted up the bids for fat cattle, or perhaps he was the kind of young pin-money aesthete who gets sucked into the proliferating departments of the great London auctioneering concerns. The latter was the more probable conjecture to the extent that Magda was what Americans call a college girl. She had got herself to Oxford—Appleby had been told—about a dozen years ago, and had there studied he didn't know what. This murky past (as it must appear to her father) suggested strength of character, or even a masterful self-will, in a Grinton, and perhaps she knew more about the Grintons than Terence Grinton did. The frequent vagueness of the armigerous classes about their own ancestry had often struck Appleby (whose own origins were distinctly modest) as among the curiosities of the English social scene.

At the moment Appleby pursued this line of thought no further. Instead, he fell to wondering how the capable but evidently perplexed Inspector Denver was now going to handle the thing. However little there was "to go on," the chap couldn't very well wash his hands of it—writing in that notebook something like, "No further action required." On the other hand he would be chary of mounting at Grinton the kind of performance which would lead to newspapers enthusiastically announcing that the police "suspected foul play," or even that they were "treating the matter as a case of murder." That way lay a quite horrific jamboree: a mobile control centre; police dogs with handlers; frogmen from the underwater search unit hunting hopefully for ponds to plunge into; files of perspiring officers apparently grazing on the lawns like transmogrified

47

sheep, but really scrabbling after nonexistent spent bullets or abandoned cigarette ends. No sensible policeman wants that sort of circus if it can possibly be avoided.

And here was a small problem for Appleby—of an ethical order, if that wasn't too elevated a term. When—in the words of the song—constabulary duty's to be done, what is the proper comportment on the part of an unconfessed constable? Appleby had sketched that provisional theory of espionage to Honeybath. Ought he at once to favour Denver with it as well? Denver hadn't asked for anything of the kind. He had scarcely had an opportunity to do so. If he had really failed to tumble to Appleby's identity, there was no particular reason for his asking questions in any case. If he *had* done so, and was making a species of solemn game out of pretending the penny hadn't dropped, perhaps he ought to be let play the thing his own way. For the time being, at least, Appleby resolved to continue lying low.

"I think we might return to the house," Denver said. "Then I'd better take formal statements from those who have been more immediately involved." He paused on this. "And see if anybody has any ideas about the thing. About just what has happened. We know that *something* has happened. And we don't know much more than that."

"Not even whether the affair's one for the police," Terence Grinton said rather surprisingly. "If there was a dead body around, you know, it would be another matter. But devil there is—unless it has been stuffed up a chimney."

"A chimney!" Honeybath exclaimed—startled by this approximation to a previous conjecture of his own.

"Or taken out and fed to the pigs." It was with a sudden and not uncharacteristic violence that Grinton loudly added this senseless conjecture. "What else, in heaven's name?"

48

"Well, sir, burglary, in a manner of speaking." Denver spoke in a deadpan respectful voice. "It's my understanding that a bed, and a table, and a cooking stove—"

"It's an interesting point." Appleby interrupted with what he judged to be a layman's innocent remark. "Does a man commit burglary by removing or proposing to remove from another man's house what he has previously planted there himself? I can imagine a whole line of magistrates urgently consulting their clerk over an issue like that."

"We can imagine a lot of things," Denver said. "It's a good deal easier than digging out facts."

This was undeniable, and produced a general silence. It prompted Appleby to a further observation.

"Or relevant facts," he said. "I rather suppose that to be the hardest task of detective officers."

"As you say, sir." Denver was again at his most wooden as he offered this concurrence. And he then led the way out of the bleakly empty room.

5

IT WAS NOW FIVE P.M. ON THE SEVENTH OF FEBRUARY, and an almanac would have provided the information that the sun was due to set in four minutes. The library at Grinton Hall seemed to be aware of something of the sort; it was turning dusky in the corners, and almost dark in those contracted spaces in which towering rows of books, monumental rather than edifying or learned in suggestion, squared up one to another in a series of bays along the north wall. Here and there in the meagre gap between these and the ceiling's gilded and convoluted cornice perched yellowed and dusty busts: Homer, Julius Caesar, obscure classical gods and goddesses. It all suddenly struck Honeybath, as the four men paused again in the middle of the room, as rather effectively sinister. He thought of those illustrations which Hablot Browne—"Phiz" to the world—could cook up for the gloomier moments in novels like *Little Dorrit* and *Bleak House.* Accusing fingers, painted or in plasterwork or marble, pointing down at sprawled and lifeless figures on shadowy floors. Generically, that kind of thing. Honeybath thought again of his projected portrait in such a grotesquely incongruous setting as that.

But this was frivolous, and he ought to be attending to what Inspector Denver was now judging it proper to say.

"Would this room be much used, sir, by your household and guests?" Denver was asking the proprietor of Grinton.

"*Used?*" What might be called Terence Grinton's King Charles's head (to continue with Dickens) was instantly touched off by the question. "Who would want to use a bloody morgue? And a morgue it has just been, according to one cock-and-bull yarn we've been listening to."

This, as uttered in Honeybath's presence, was scarcely urbane. But Denver gave no sign of disapproval—which wouldn't, indeed, have been his place. He did, however, appear interested. To Appleby, whose resolve to be unobtrusive didn't prevent his being other than a keen observer of whatever was going on, it had already seemed that Denver was distinctly interested in the violent Terence. He had been shooting keen sidelong glances at him from time to time.

"And we'd better get out of the place," Grinton said, and moved towards the door.

But Denver didn't budge. It was something he would be good at, Appleby thought, when still uncertain of any direction in which to move.

"Just so," Denver said—much as if something prosaically sensible had just been said. "And it occurs to me that this library, being not otherwise required, may be the best place for me to set up in."

"*To set up in?*" Grinton might have been listening to astounding words. "What the devil do you mean?" That Inspector Denver had performed meritorious services in marching off those pestilent yatterers on cruel blood sports was now far from the mind of the Master of the Nether Barset Hunt. "If you ask me, Denver, you'd better cut off and turn in a report to the Chief Constable. Something of that kind."

"I'm afraid that's not exactly the position, sir. You called in the police—"

"The deuce I did!" Grinton spoke with every appearance of honest indignation. That it was he who had directed his wife to ask for the meritorious Denver might have been as remote from his consciousness as was the present political situation in Kamchatka.

"And very properly, sir, in my judgement. The situation is certainly a little obscure, but there is at least some reason to believe that there has been a theft of your property."

"A theft of my property!" Grinton looked extremely startled. "What the deuce do you mean, Denver?"

"A table, chair, and other effects. It is reasonable to suppose that what Sir John Appleby and Mr. Honeybath came upon in there formed part of your household goods. I noticed one or two similar articles through the open door of another of those small rooms. But now these particular articles have been removed without the knowledge of their owner—to wit, yourself, sir. So burglary must be suspected. Burglary is a serious offence in itself, irrespective of the scale of the felony envisaged. Police investigation is essential."

Honeybath, whose profession rendered him perforce a student of character, felt instructed by his prospective sitter's reception of this not altogether plausible speech. Grinton was perceiving that it required thought. And Grinton resented this. He was not a thoughtful man. Thought was an activity which, steadily over the years, he had been addressing himself with some success to doing without. So he naturally resented any sudden call for its employment. This state of mind (if the expression was appropriate) struck Honeybath as an interesting one to pursue on the part of a portrait painter. For the first time at Grinton he felt a strong impulse to get to work. Thus he too rather resented Denver as now an obstinate presence in the place. Unlike John Appleby, he was coming to regard the whole business of the corpse and its vanishing trick as vexatious rather than interesting. It was not the less vexatious for having been hinted to him by Appleby as something that was going to occasion him a good deal of harassment at the hands of this conscientious officer.

"Look here!" Grinton was saying violently. "If you were sent for, it certainly wasn't on account of some confounded tables and chairs. There are more than enough of the damned things about the house, and if a few have been pinched by some prowling prole I couldn't care less." Terence Grinton paused on these reflections, and seemed faintly aware of them as a little lacking in relevance. "It's what Mr. Honeybath here saw, or thought he saw, that has brought you in on us, Denver. You know that perfectly well. So if you can just clear up that bit of twaddle, and then take yourself off, I'll be grateful to you."

This was undoubtedly a very rude speech, yet not without a gleam of reason. And Denver received it without any token of offence.

"Quite so, sir. Only you see, dealing with that aspect of the situation may take a little time. A start, however, can be made at once. My officers will have arrived by now."

"Your officers! Who the hell are they?"

"Two experienced and reliable men, I'm glad to say. They will act as unobtrusively as may be—only you must understand that they may have to do a good deal of ferreting around. That is unavoidable."

"Ferreting, you say?" The word had the unexpected effect of appearing to bring Grinton within familiar and therefore comprehensible territory. He was perhaps recalling that his son-in-law and grandchildren were out with a ferret at that moment. "Well, we'll leave you to it. And here in the library, if that's your fancy. You'll want to question the servants, no doubt."

"That may come in time, sir. But it will be best to begin with your family and guests—asking everybody in an orderly way, you know, if they have any light to throw on the situation. And taking evidence, as I've said, from those more evidently involved. Preferably one by one, and dictating statements which can then be read over and signed. Entirely a matter of voluntary cooperation at this stage, I need hardly say. And I'll begin with Mr. Honeybath, if he will oblige."

Unavoidably, Mr. Honeybath obliged—and thus found himself alone with Denver in no time at all.

"A difficult man," Denver said.

"I beg your pardon?"

"Mr. Grinton. A tetchy chap."

Honeybath found he didn't at all know how to respond to this familiar note. It was scarcely proper to concur enthusiastically in such a verdict upon one's host. On the other hand, *tetchy* was an expressive English word of which he approved, and there could be no doubt whatever as to its applicability.

"True enough," he said. "And something I have to take an interest in. I'm here to paint his portrait."

"Quite so, sir." Denver opened his notebook and brought out his pen, as if formal proceedings were now to begin. "Mr. Charles Honeybath," he said—and appeared to write down the name. "R.A., I think it would be?"

54

"Yes." Honeybath, whose boyhood had been lived amid dreams of artistic glory, took no particular pride in the indubitable distinction of being a Royal Academician.

"Interesting. They say, you know, that the Grintons are uncommonly hard up. Vanity, would you say?"

It took Honeybath a moment to catch on to the sense of this. It was simply that Terence Grinton's financial situation was such as to render a portrait an injudicious luxury, and that vanity was perhaps the explanation. Honeybath was quite clear that it would be wholly improper to volunteer the information that the portrait was to be paid for by subscription—a fact which couldn't possibly be of any relevance to the messy business of the vanishing corpse.

"I don't think I'd call Mr. Grinton vain," he said briefly. But he did wonder whether it might be true that the family was short of money. Terence couldn't conceivably be *earning* money; the company didn't exist that would pay him a fee to sit on its board. And there was no positive reason to suppose that behind him there any longer stood substantial inherited wealth. He probably blundered along as a landowner, and that was it. But here again was something irrelevant to that corpse.

"And now to get down to it," Denver said comfortably. "It seems to me, sir, that we are on rather surer ground through that dummy door than we are here in the library. It's not that I don't judge your evidence to be reliable in every way. But you were on your own when you came upon this seemingly dead man. And you came away fairly quickly. I can imagine you in a witness-box, Mr. Honeybath, being cross-examined by counsel defending some villain or other. He might get some way in persuading a jury that there wasn't all that evidence that the dead man wasn't presently able to get up and walk. But it's different when we get through that fake door. Sir John Appleby is with you when you are on the other side of it. Of course it's quite irrelevant that Sir John has been the Metropolitan Commissioner." Denver said this positively airily. "It's simply that two are better than one when a witness-box is in prospect. I hope, sir, you follow me."

"Of course I follow you." Honeybath wondered whether "testy" could fairly be applied to his manner of saying this.

"Well, sir, your statement needn't take us five minutes. I've a very fair notion of its content already. But I do wonder whether you have formed any impression about the whole thing."

"I have been thinking about it, of course." Honeybath recalled Appleby's advice to refrain from conjectures. "But not, I'm afraid, to any effect worth recording. I'm entirely in the dark. Probably a good deal more than you are."

"Well, sir. I don't mind admitting that, for a start, I'd like a little more light on that dead body. You are convinced that it *was* a dead body, and would maintain that in court. Right?"

"Certainly." Honeybath hesitated. "But you might call that my rational conviction. It has been dawning on me that, in a position like mine, it isn't easy to be wholeheartedly rational. Really, I begin to harbour doubts. Coma, now. One hears a lot about coma nowadays. How close to actual death can its appearances be?"

"Deep waters, Mr. Honeybath. It used to be assumed that death invariably happens in a breath. One moment alive; the next, not. Nowadays there's a different view. And whether this man was really dead is something—to be frank with you—that I have to keep an open mind about. But of one thing I'm confident. If he was merely in deep coma when you came on him, he could nevertheless be in no condition simply to stand up and walk out of the room a few minutes later. Alive or dead, he was carried out. Somebody lugged the guts into the neighbour room."

This literary flight on the part of Inspector Denver quite startled Honeybath. But he saw that a real analysis was going forward.

"There's another question," Denver said. "Agree that you were correct in deciding the man was dead. Did any suggestion of the cause of death occur to you then and there?"

"I'm afraid it didn't. I can't recall holding any internal debate on the matter." Honeybath was aware of this as rather a pedantic form of words. "But you see what that means," he suddenly added. "I must have been taking it for granted that the chap had just died in a perfectly natural manner. As Appleby has pointed out to me, most people do. And at times very suddenly, if I'm not mistaken. A totally unheralded cerebral disaster. One has been harbouring a treacherous aneurysm—I believe that's the word—inside one's head, and quite suddenly it goes bust."

"But you didn't, at the time, actually find yourself thinking along those lines?"

"Assuredly not. I was simply extremely shocked."

"Quite so, Mr. Honeybath. Nothing could be more natural. Of course if you had happened to think of something entirely different—some form of violent death, I mean—you would probably have spared a moment or two to investigate before going for help."

"No doubt. And if there had been any substantial and overt sign of violence I'd surely have been aware of it. If the man was murdered, in other words, it wasn't in any strikingly gory fashion."

"Exactly. No blood here, and none next door—where you and Sir John had those two odd experiences."

"*Two* experiences?"

"Oh, decidedly. Signs of an unobtrusive squatter in a country house like Grinton were uncommonly curious in themselves. And then finding that the signs had vanished was more curious still."

"A vagrant," Honeybath said hopefully. "A kind of new style tramp. Or an enterprising hippie, perhaps with a little van. He has been quite snug here. But something sinister happens, and he takes alarm and bolts."

"Dear me!" Denver was staring at Honeybath in what might have been charitably regarded as admiring astonishment. "I'd almost suppose you to be a scientist, sir, rather than an artist. I believe fertility in the field of hypothesis to be the hallmark of your top scientific man." Having allowed himself this frivolity, Denver again took up his pen. "Just a brief recital of facts," he said. "That you can put your signature to. Not a deposition, you understand, in any legal sense. Just to help us along."

Honeybath helped along, and then withdrew from the library. His own duty in the matter he could now consider to have been discharged, and it was unlikely that anyone would bother him again. Nevertheless he continued to feel something vexatious about the whole affair. He had come to Grinton to cope with a mystery, since that is what painting the portrait of another human being involves. Or painting a kitchen chair or an old pair of boots for that matter. You have to love the things, and achieve an obscure act of possession, and the result is that you have brought a minute speck of light into the vast darkness in which we move and have our being. Honeybath had preserved this sober faith in his craft through several decades of painting Terence Grintons and Dolly Grintons and all their company. So it was tiresome that when just about to start on a serious job there should bob up this distracting issue of a mobile corpse.

He had left Denver sitting in the library, absorbed in pen-and-ink labours like some conscientious fellow in what they called middle management. Honeybath felt that the man ought to be on the telephone arranging a sort of cordon of roadblocks round Grinton, or out and about in the shrubberies hunting for clues with a magnifying glass. But perhaps his subordinates were now doing that sort of thing. Perhaps Denver was like a spider, alert at the centre of a finely fabricated web of intelligence. He didn't quite give that impression. But no doubt he was competent enough.

The broad corridor from the library led to the main hall of the house. This had at some time or other been carved out of several rooms, so that both in its shape and in its proportions it was a little odd. But it was spacious and also lofty, since a couple of upstairs bedrooms had disappeared into it as well. It testified to the consequence of the Grintons; its walls were adorned with trophies of the chase; it had been furnished in a half-hearted way as a place to sit about in.

Nobody was sitting in it now. But at one end, and beside the door leading to a vestibule, there stood a uniformed policeman. Although he rendered no impression of being aggressively immobile, and although the epithet "rigid" could scarcely be applied to him, he was yet so motionless, so little suggestive of having lately done anything or of being about to do something, that he somehow seemed less a policeman than what is called a police presence. Within a fairly short span of time the entire Grinton family and their guests were almost sure to pass through this hall. Honeybath therefore concluded that the role of this constable (who was "stolid" as all such persons are in fiction) was simply to impress the household at large with the reserve, the lurking, powers of the law.

The Applebys now appeared—Judith presumably having lately returned in the dusk from a long tramp on the downs. For a moment they didn't notice Honeybath. Appleby strolled up to the constable just as if he were quite real but also entirely harmless. The constable appreciated this, producing brisk and amiable replies to whatever Appleby was saying to him. Judith began to circle the hall, pausing here and there before masks and brushes as if some interesting individuality attached to one vulpine relic or another. Then she saw Honeybath and came over to him.

"Charles," she said, "John has just spun me the most extraordinary yarn about high jinks at Grinton. I suppose it's not one of his tiresome jokes?"

"Definitely not. I've no doubt he has told you exactly what has happened—or the very little that we *know* to have happened, perhaps I'd better say."

"You didn't do it, Charles?"

"Judith!"

"I expect it's what everybody's going to be asked—if not just in so many words. John says one reading of the thing is murder of someone unknown by someone unknown. One must hope it turns out to be an inside job."

"I sometimes can't decide whether you or John is the sillier." Honeybath had known Judith from childhood.

"There would be more excitement in an inside job. Haven't you even been *suspected?*"

"Well, I've just come from an interview with the top policeman on the scene. Whether he suspects me or not, I haven't the faintest idea. But it's his business to suspect everybody, no doubt. Although of precisely what isn't yet at all clear."

"John says he's next after you for interview. Here he is."

Appleby, having finished his conversation with the constable, had now joined them.

"Yes, it's me next," he said cheerfully. "And do you know? I don't believe this excellent Denver has a clue to my murky past."

"Ah!" It was plain that Honeybath relished this. And he was even constrained to an uncustomary colloquial note. "John," he said, "don't make me laugh."

6

"I HOPE I GUESSED RIGHT," DENVER SAID TO APPLEBY.
"About not wanting your official position brought forward,
that is."

"My former official position, Mr. Denver. But you were
certainly right. I know very little about most of the people
now at Grinton, and some of them might quite well take it
into their heads that I was ready to meddle in this thing.
Nothing could be further from the truth."

"Quite so, Sir John."

"And for that matter, you know, retired or not retired is
all one. If the present Metropolitan Commissioner—a very
nice fellow, by the way—was in this house now, he would
have no special standing in the matter whatever."

"Very true, indeed, sir, speaking by the book."

"Well, let me make that statement for you. At four thirty-
five this afternoon I was about to enter the drawing room at
Grinton Hall. I met my fellow guest, Mr. Charles Honeybath, coming out. Mr. Honeybath said, 'John! There's a
dead man in the library.' I said—"

Appleby was speaking at brisk dictation speed, so Denver had to grab his pen and make do. For two or three
minutes he scribbled hard.

"Read it back to me," Appleby then said, "and I'll sign

and you can get on to your next chap. Grinton himself, I suppose."

"Yes—Grinton." Denver didn't seem enchanted with the professional brevity of this performance; in fact, he looked very like a man who wants to say, "But please don't go away." What he did say was, "Mr. Honeybath tells me he's painting his portrait. He's rather a tetchy fellow."

"Mr. Honeybath?"

"No, sir. Mr. Grinton." Denver was unruffled. "Would you have known him for long?"

"For a good many years, in a very slight way. Through some female line or other, he's related remotely to my wife. On two or three occasions we've lunched at Grinton. But this is our first regular visit."

"Have you noticed, Sir John, anything odd about Mr. Grinton's attitude to this room?"

"My dear Denver, I've had very little time to become aware of anything of the sort. But, I suppose, in a way— yes. It's no more than goes with a certain general eccentricity of character. Plenty of people, you know, don't care much for book learning. It just doesn't enter their lives. But that perfectly common trait Grinton seems to carry a step further. He positively dislikes books, and so owns a frank antipathy to his own library."

"More than that, Sir John. He keeps people out of it. There's something almost nervous about the thing. And progressively so."

"I've had no opportunity to remark that, Inspector. And I don't see how you can have had such an opportunity either. To observe, I mean, any change of attitude or emphasis on Mr. Grinton's part."

"Well, not myself, sir. Certainly not. But I've had a word with the butler."

"The dickens you have!" Appleby was impressed by this.

"I got hold of him by saying I'd need him to hunt up people I wanted to talk to. It wouldn't have been colourable, of course, to have more than five minutes' chat with him. But I told him he mustn't be surprised if one of my men turned up in this library with a little vacuum cleaner. It would be to collect specimens of dust for scientific purposes. There was a surprising amount of dust, I said. That touched his professional pride. Nowadays—as you must have noticed in your walk of life, Sir John—a butler is often the only upper servant even in rather grand places like this one. He doubles up as housekeeper as well, and is in charge of the entire bag of tricks, you may say. Well, the man explained to me that Mr. Grinton can hardly have anybody enter this library—and he says this seems to have been particularly true of late." Denver glanced quickly at Appleby; he probably felt that he had got his man. "It takes some accounting for, if you ask me."

"Are you suggesting, Inspector, that this room harbours a dark secret, which an intruder might stumble upon? A mad relation, perhaps, dressed chiefly in rags and cobwebs?"

"Not quite that, Sir John." Denver was again unruffled in the face of this mockery. "But, well—something."

"Then why doesn't Grinton simply keep the room locked up?"

"That would perhaps be a little too obtrusive to be prudent."

"If he said his library happens to contain items of great value, turning a key on it might seem quite natural. But I don't say you're not on to something, Denver. Well within a target area. We have to keep thinking about this room." Appleby was aware that he had employed a possibly disastrous pronoun. "Whenever you think about that dead body, think about this room as well. And now I'd better make way for your next suspect."

"There's one thing Grinton can't be suspected of." Denver gave no sign he felt this interview to be over. "Shunting the body—always supposing it *was* a body, of which I'm not quite convinced—through that dummy door. He was in the drawing room as that was happening."

"So it would seem. But that sort of alibi, you know, can turn out to be unexpectedly tricky." Appleby was now the man of experience, uttering cautionary words. "Have an incident reenacted as closely as may be, keep a stopwatch in your hand, and surprising results sometimes appear."

"Of course that's so. And it would be absurd to speak of Mr. Grinton as a suspect, anyway." Denver somehow didn't say this very convincingly. "Far too many unknown quantities still. For the sheer devil of the thing, give me what they call a house party every time."

"Well, yes. But it isn't a *big* house party, you know. And it's not really a very big house either. Think if this was happening at Blenheim or Knole or Castle Howard."

"Or Scamnum Court," Denver said—thus showing a surprising acquaintance with Appleby's early career. "But you know, sir, there is one promising factor in this affair. It's rum. It's uncommonly rum—and that's something. Because, you know, it's when one has an absolutely colourless crime—"

"There's been a crime?" Appleby interrupted. "Apart from that absurd talk you put up about burglared furniture?"

"I think there's been a crime." Denver said this with a very proper gravity. "But what I was suggesting is this: it's the colourless crime that can be the devil to get any grip on. As soon as the quirky comes in, there's likely to be something to get hold of."

"That's very true." Appleby contrived to receive with admiring surprise this commonplace of criminological lore.

"So concentrate on the very odd business of a dead man being spirited away. Tabulate all rational motives for such an act that you can think of, and then weigh each in turn."

"But are there *any* rational motives? Can you come up with one for a start, Sir John?" Denver seemed to feel that this had been venturesome. "For I don't know that I can," he added.

"Well now, what about it's being a matter of taste?"

"Taste, Sir John?"

"There's a certain suggestion that a dead body had been perched or posed in that chair to create a macabre effect upon discovery. The perpetrator may have decided, upon reflection, that it was a somewhat unbecoming joke. Not on, as they say. So he picked up the corpse again and moved elsewhere."

Inspector Denver—as well he might—didn't at once know how to take this.

"Would you really think—" he began.

"I'm not being entirely frivolous. In cases of murder—and we keep an open mind about this being one—the murderer often turns curiously confused. He may go in for compunctions before the deed, but something like mere bewilderment after it. The classical instance is Shakespeare's Macbeth."

"Macbeth's bewilderment wouldn't have caused him to move Duncan's body out of the chamber where he'd murdered him." Denver, a reasonably literate man, remembered the play pretty clearly. "Lady Macbeth might have done it—if she'd seen any sense in so doing."

"Excellent! You see how indulging in quite fanciful ideas can open up useful trains of thought."

"You mean, sir, that Mrs. Grinton, as well as Grinton himself, may have been in on the act?"

66

Appleby, not commonly unready in reply, was held up for a moment by this. He wondered whether Dolly Grinton could possibly support the character of a fiendlike queen. More clearly, he saw that the otherwise thoroughly competent Inspector was in some danger of developing an awkward *idée fixe* about Terence Grinton. Terence had undoubtedly been uncivil to the chap. But Terence would be uncivil to anybody, and with a kind of saving geniality more often than not. Appleby wondered whether he ought to try to put in a good word for Terence. But then he remembered that he had been asked a question and had better answer it.

"It certainly hasn't occurred to me, Denver, to start suspecting my host and hostess of some dark crime. I meant merely that there may be two or more villains in the piece. Two people, for that matter, can lug a body around more easily than one." Appleby hesitated for a moment. "But just go back to that rather odd thing you said about Grinton. Surely you've already admitted that as a prime suspect he just doesn't stand up. When this supposed body-shunting business was going on, he was at the other end of the house."

"Yes, Sir John, we've just taken account of that—and it was you yourself who had a cautionary word about alibis. It's no more than that I feel Mr. Grinton is somehow keeping something or other in the bag. And it might be quite natural that his wife should know about it."

"I wouldn't dispute the general proposition that husbands and wives have a tendency to share secrets. If you are a married man yourself, you know that very well."

"Yes, indeed, sir. And would you be inclined to say that of those two it's the lady who is the brighter by some way?"

"Perhaps so." Appleby wasn't quite comfortable before

this turn in the discussion of the persons whose hospitality he was enjoying. But the feeling was one it would be quite wrong to give weight to. "Estimating intelligence is a tricky thing, Inspector, as you know very well. Mrs. Grinton is certainly clever, but I'm not at all clear that Mr. Grinton is stupid."

"Cunning, perhaps?"

This looked like the *idée fixe* again, and Appleby paused before coping with it.

"When intelligence and lack of information go together," he said, "an effect of cunning is sometimes the result. And I would say of Grinton—without in the least wanting to disparage the man—that he is quite surprisingly ignorant about a great deal."

"And the sort that, if he *can* get something wrong, *will* get it wrong?"

"An extreme view, perhaps—and I don't really know him anything like well enough to say. But I certainly wouldn't—well—trust him with the conduct of my affairs. And now, Inspector, you'd better have your own little chat with him."

Charles Honeybath, meanwhile, had wandered back to the drawing room. It was the violet hour, when—as the poet says—the eyes and back turn upward from the desk. Honeybath had no desk, and at the moment not even an easel. He was finding the violet hour unsatisfactory—as it can often be in an English country house in what is still late winter rather than early spring. Women talk about gardening, but without conviction; men grumble because they are no longer allowed to shoot things—unless, indeed, there are duck around; children, bundled out of school on the pretext of a "half-term" exeat, are troublesome presences.

It may be more than an hour before a bell rings by way of telling you to get out of one set of clothes and into another: a ritual pleasing to the female sex but rather boring to the male. And quite often you are lucky if you so much as get a drink in advance of the announcement that dinner is served.

Honeybath had missed his tea, and although nothing of the sort was still likely to be going on, there might yet be a stray uncleared sandwich to nibble. It turned out there was a little more: a teapot on a stand, and a tiny blue flame under a kettle. Nor was the drawing room entirely untenanted. Two other guests were in possession: the man called Hallam Hillam, and Grinton's son-in-law, Giles Tancock. They seemed to have been conferring together as Honeybath entered the room. The afternoon's sensational event must by now be known throughout the household, and no doubt there was much to be conjectured about it. Honeybath himself had in a sense been the hero of the occasion, so perhaps these two men would question him about it. He didn't want this. He didn't feel he knew either at all well, and he had an uncertain sense of their owning some common world only in a tenuous relationship with his own. It seemed necessary to make an attempt at conversation.

"How did it go with the rabbits?" he asked Tancock.

"The rabbits?" For a moment Tancock stared at him vacantly. "Oh, that! I left them to it, with their mum to make sure the boy didn't blow his sister's brains out, and I just prowled around. In the dirt, you know—for dirt's the right word for most of the Grinton land. Not even muck, for which there's something to be said. Just dirt. How any rent at all can be raised from it is beyond me. Of course there are those louts with motorbikes and bashed up stock cars. They could drive all over the estate having rallies and things, and perhaps drop a copper or two into the kitty. It would all help."

Honeybath, because he judged this to be a disobliging and indeed graceless speech, left it without rejoinder. But he remembered Denver's suggestion that the Grintons were hard up. This chatter about worthless or neglected land seemed to be in the same area. He devoted himself to peering into the teapot, pouring out an experimental cup of what it contained, and picking up a biscuit. He glanced at Hillam, and found that nothing came into his head to say to the man. He remembered that earlier in the afternoon Hillam had in some trifling way been uncivil to him, and also that the fellow had come out with a rather lewd joke. But these recollections failed to prompt conversation, and it was Hillam who now spoke.

"Tancock and I have been talking about this extraordinary affair in the library," he said. "It begins to look as if it was right to regard it as an affair for the police. I'm afraid I treated it with a certain levity earlier on."

"It's the sort of thing that can throw one off one's stride for a time." Honeybath made this rather meaningless remark by way of acknowledging that Hillam had been offering some kind of *amende honorable*. "There's no easy sense to be made of it. Appleby and that local police chief are chewing over it in the library now."

"From what I hear," Tancock said, "the only explanation seems to be that there has been some sort of lunatic around the place. A particularly crazy variety of recluse. Quartering himself in some corner of the house nobody ever goes near, and varying that with spells in the library. Of course nobody ever goes near the library either. But how would a wandering zany know that? The thing's senseless."

"What you describe would be senseless in itself," Honeybath said. "But there's more to it than that. It looks like two unaccountable presences rather than one." He drank his tepid tea. "And it rather looks as if—" He broke off and reached hastily for another biscuit. Appleby's theory of clandestine literary research was much in his mind, and he had been within an ace of embarking upon it in the way of mere gossip with these two almost unknown men. "It looks rather as if the explanation of the mystery may be hard to seek."

"And be best left to the professionals," Hillam said helpfully. It was as if Hillam, although by nature disagreeable, had decided that in the present state of affairs at Grinton some sort of amenity of address was the prudent thing.

"Oh, I don't know as to that." Giles Tancock was now lounging in front of a bright fire, but at the same time shifting his weight restlessly from foot to foot. "God knows, this house is uncommonly dull. Dolly does her best—and I make Magda back her up—to press-gang into Grinton an occasional character with something between the ears other than solid bone. But it's hard going. So an incident in the briskly criminal way might liven us up. Just reflect on my father-in-law's common conversation. He's a decent old ruffian, I don't deny, and even quite endearing in his way. But his talk—well, God save my whiskers!" Upon this unusual pious ejaculation, Tancock turned to Honeybath. "Have you heard him on his rates and taxes?"

Honeybath had, in fact, heard Terence Grinton on this theme—already more than once. Nevertheless he said instantly, "No, I have not." It seemed to him the best means of marking his strong disapproval of the tone in which Grinton's son-in-law spoke.

"There's a kind of persecution mania at the bottom of it," Tancock said confidently. "I happen to know that Terence has a perfectly competent accountant. In fact, I made Magda find him for the old boy. But he still believes that he's put upon by villainous and faceless creatures in the Inland Revenue."

"It's a very common attitude," Hillam said on his new composing note. "A very easy persuasion to fall into. But it's true that Grinton does talk about it rather a lot. So the mysterious affair in the library may be a welcome change, I agree. I do wonder, however, whether one ought perhaps to go away."

"What do you mean—go away?"

"Well, of course, you're a member of the family, Tancock, and that's different. But I have a notion that when there's been a fatality in a household—or anything serious, you know, of that kind—it's perhaps the proper thing for mere casual guests to terminate their visit as unobtrusively as may be."

"Unobtrusively? Packing a bag and levanting in the middle of the night? You'd have the fuzz after you in no time." Tancock backed this up with a contemptuous laugh, as if Hillam were an absurd person who went about with a book on etiquette in his baggage. Honeybath's sympathies were rather with Hillam, who had raised an issue not wholly without substance. Imagine, for example, Terence Grinton breaking his neck (which he might do on any three or four days out of seven) and it would surely be incumbent upon persons congregated in the dead man's house for mere routine jollification to mutter appropriate words and clear out. On the other hand it would be absurd to do anything of the kind if—say—the body of some unfortunate mendicant had been found in a woodshed. The status of what had been found (and quickly lost) at Grinton was still an entirely unknown quantity.

"At least Honeybath can't pack his bag," Tancock said to Hillam, seemingly with intent to continue in a humorous vein. "He has a job to do, and a cheque to collect. But where shall the thing hang? Honeybath, have you tackled my mother-in-law about that? She'll decide, you know. You must have noticed already that Dolly runs the Grinton circus."

"I've had no discussion about it with Mrs. Grinton or anybody else," Honeybath said. "There are former Grintons here and there around the house. Some of them are rather good—although none that I've noticed is by a painter of any great celebrity. I expect a niche for my effort will be found somewhere."

"But not in here," Hillam said. "Anything of the kind would look uncommonly odd."

"True enough." Tancock glanced not very attentively round the room. "It's a curious thing about drawing rooms in a house like this. The lady's word is law in it—and generation by generation a new lady arrives who has at least a slightly different background behind her. But she sets no fresh mark on the place. And Dolly isn't an exception. Long ago, she created a room for herself upstairs, then all very new and *à la mode*. But this drawing room has remained as undisturbed—well—as the library itself. Those silhouette things festooning the fireplace. And all the watercolour sketches perpetrated by all the Grinton females that ever were. And there are thousands of similar family mausoleums all over England. Terrifying."

Charles Honeybath, who believed that any setting of brush or pencil to paper whether by man, woman or child partook of the sanctity of creation, was not disposed to feel terrified. On the contrary, he was prompted to circle the room and inspect the artistic labours of the ladies invoked.

They were certainly daunting in quantity, and in quality most of them were, of course, insipid enough. Grinton Hall, its perspectives very shakily perceived, figured in a good many. So did approved "beauty spots" in Scotland and Switzerland. In fact you might say that there was much social history on the walls.

"As always," Honeybath said, "it's possible to spot one or two ladies in whom untutored talent lurks. Somebody was obsessed by an oak tree struck by lightning, and goes at it again and again. And—by Jove!—here she brings it off." Honeybath was as pleased as if this success had been achieved by his own daughter. "But here's something different. *Quite* different. Not the Grinton *atelier* at all. Look, Tancock! Just a cottage and a tree and a boat on a stream— as unassuming a little thing as you please. But it's certainly by John Varley, and both Blake and Palmer are hovering in it. Wouldn't you say?" Honeybath was quite unconscious of the fact that Tancock might know nothing of these things. "The tub is floating past on invisible water. That's time. And the tree is just coming into leaf again. Life eternal. A wonderful little thing."

"Nobody would give more than a couple of hundred pounds for it," Hillam said.

"I suppose not." Honeybath was still too pleased by the small sketch to be bothered by this tasteless remark. "Odd that it should turn up in the middle of all this family piety. Let's see if there's anything else."

Honeybath moved on. Tancock, who had approached and looked at the Varley with civil interest, turned back and took up his position before the fire again, apparently feeling that an adequate polite gesture had been made. Hillam made to follow Honeybath, but paused suddenly in the middle of the room.

"I say, Honeybath!" he said. "Just come and look at these—in this glass-topped affair. There must have been a nabob among the Grintons at one time or other. And with an eye for such things. Superb little bronzes. Just look at that high-kicking Nataraja. And the Pattini Devi. It's as fine as the larger one in the B.M. Good Lord! A Swat Valley figure of Tathagata Aksobhya. Ninth century, I'd say."

Honeybath examined the small collection of Indian divinities with respect. It certainly made an odd outcrop of the exotic in this commonplace English drawing room. And odd, too, was Hillam's sudden enthusiasm—apparently an informed enthusiasm. He was scarcely the same man who had offered some merely crass remark before the Varley. And then Honeybath remembered that the man curated something. Perhaps it was Eastern Antiquities. Honeybath didn't know much about that field, and would have said that he preferred a single George Stubbs horse (even if being devoured by a lion) to a whole troop of sacred elephants. But one ought always to be willing to learn, and it is pleasant suddenly to discover in a favourable light somebody whom one has been tempted to regard as rather a tiresome fellow. So for some minutes he listened to instructive remarks about Buddhas and Bodhisattvas. And then that bell went to tell people to go and dress.

7

IN SPITE OF THE AGITATIONS OF THE AFTERNOON AT GRIN-
ton, there turned out to be a properly attended quarter of
an hour for the purpose of drinking sherry before dinner.
For some reason it was a ritual somewhat formally conceived—the stuff being taken round by Burrow on a salver
rather than simply being poured out by Terence Grinton or
by oneself. The method, it struck Appleby, had a certain
effect of controlling the amount consumed, and might have
been devised by Dolly Grinton in the interest either of
sobriety or economy. Perhaps her husband or her son-in-
law inclined to the bad habit of sitting down at table already
well lit up. Or perhaps quite small expenditures had to be
kept an eye on throughout the entire Grinton economy.
Appleby had recently read that it cost eighty pounds a
week to feed an elephant in the zoo. If the Nether Barset
was conducted on somewhat old-fashioned lines—which he
didn't at all know—and its Master expected to provide
most of the board and lodging for a large pack of hounds, it
might well be that Dolly had to own a constant regard for
the *res angusta domi*.

If so, it certainly didn't get her down. After her own
fashion—an extremely cheerful one—she was almost as as-

sertive as her husband. She was advancing on Appleby now, holding up her little sherry glass as extravagantly as if it had been a beaker full of the warm South.

"John," she said familiarly, "you are the exception. I declare you to be the sole exception. You may sleep in the house or spend the night prowling through the house, but you will be the only policeman to do so. I told that Mr. Denver to go away."

"And he went?"

"Indeed he went, and took his small change—his junior coppers, that is—with him." Perhaps through long cohabitation with Terence, Dolly had the habit of elucidating her own jokes as she went along. "Of course I told him very nicely, and he made no fuss at all."

"I see. And just what has he done about the library?"

"*Done* about the library? Why nothing at all. Why should he?"

"I thought it possible he might want to lock it up—just in case his back-room boys want to give it a go-through tomorrow."

"A go-through? Don't be absurd, John. It would take the entire county constabulary a month to do anything of the sort."

"Well, in one sense—yes. But considering that Charles Honeybath . . ." Appleby was about to add something like "found a dead man there," but wasn't given the chance.

"Dear Mr. Honeybath!" Dolly broke in—with something like a Terence laugh in a minor mode. "He ought to have been a visionary painter, like poor dear Marc Chagall. What fun his Terence would be then."

Appleby made no reply to this—and indeed any rational response wouldn't have been easy. That the library at Grinton had returned *in pristinum statum*—to wit, a room into which it just so happened one didn't go—struck him as a shade unaccountable. But he was far from feeling that Inspector Denver didn't know his business, and police methods had no doubt refined themselves since his own day. As for Dolly Grinton, she had apparently decided to believe that Honeybath's report of finding a corpse was akin to the discovery by occasional disordered persons that little green men had arrived from the moon. And to this view Appleby ventured on an oblique challenge.

"I hope," he said seriously, "you're not going to miss the articles of furniture that Honeybath and I came on in that room beyond the library, and that disappeared so rapidly thereafter."

"Oh, that!" For a moment Dolly Grinton was a little at a loss, since she could not very directly suggest that Appleby was in the habit of spotting little green men too. "The servants are always shifting their own bits and pieces around. Something of that kind. Will you have another glass of sherry? But—how very tiresome!—Burrow has gone away. He'll be giving us his shout at any moment. I do hope there's a decent meal. Terence is less disagreeable when he has been well fed. Just like the hounds." Dolly set down her glass on the showcase sheltering the Indian divinities, and they perhaps prompted her next remark. "Hallam Hillam," she said. "I suppose you've had some conversation with him by this time. Don't you find him a quite fascinating man?"

"I'm aware of something interesting about him." There was nobody at Grinton at the moment about whom Appleby might not have offered this temperate statement. "Is he an old friend of yours?"

"Not remotely!" Dolly picked up her glass again, simply for the purpose of giving a small airy wave with it. "I met him at a party somewhere no time ago, and he talked in the

78

most marvellous way about burning ghats and things of that sort."

"That's his line, is it: Indian religions, and so on?"

"No, it seems to be just a hobby. Hillam has the most wonderful breadth of mind. He says that he's by profession an iconographer. That means Russian, I suppose. It's the Russians, isn't it, who go in for icons and the like?"

"Certainly it is. But I rather believe that an iconographer is something a little different. He occupies a specific corner in the general field of the history of the figurative arts." Appleby was conscious that this speech, although reasonably concise, had been a little heavily informative for a preprandial occasion. "So you struck up an acquaintance-ship," he said, "and invited Mr. Hillam down for the weekend?"

"Not exactly that. He simply wrote and proposed himself. It was so charmingly unconventional! He said he had enjoyed our chat."

"Dinner is served, madam!"

Dolly Grinton touched Appleby on the arm. It might almost have been a tap with a fan.

"I've put you beside Kate Arne," she said. "Such an interesting old soul! She was my daughter Magda's tutor at Somerville."

The world's population, Appleby thought, was aging even more rapidly than the great globe itself. In the "Deaths" column of newspapers circulating among the more prosperous classes people were ceasing to record the tale of years to which a parent or grandparent or great-grandparent had attained, as if positively ashamed that a member of the family should have cumbered the earth so long. Even among those vast populations of "undeveloped" countries hovering on the verge of starvation infants were surviving a

79

few more months into childhood than in unhappier times, and this pushed up the average age of living people as a whole. In England it might be said that he and his neighbour Miss Arne had already joined the Great Majority, if by that term might be understood persons retired from active life.

Miss Arne, indeed, looked fit for a good deal of activity yet. She must already have been a very senior Oxford don when Magda Grinton's tutor, but she bore every appearance of being able, at need, to put young people through it still—or elderly people too, for the matter of that.

"It is no doubt the understood thing," Miss Arne said briskly, "that we don't sit round this table and gossip about the obscure event of the afternoon. Even when sitting beside such an authority on low life and criminal practice as Sir John Appleby."

Appleby judged that "low life and criminal practice" was legitimated in Miss Arne's eyes as being a quotation of which he ought to be able to identify the literary source. He also judged that in conversation with Miss Arne it was necessary to pull one's socks up.

"Gracious lady," he said firmly, "I have no evidence that anything largely criminal has occurred at Grinton, although there have certainly been some policemen around. And I believe—although I am not sure that the police do—that somebody has died. But I do agree with you that the facts, meagre as they are, suggest little that can properly be gossiped about."

"Then, Sir John, we must find some other field of joint interest. There are the Grintons, who have so agreeably brought us together. But I suppose one doesn't anatomize common friends when actually at their board."

"Well, no—I suppose not. Not Grintons present, but what about Grintons past? That would be fair enough, and I believe the family history might interest me. How about Magda's knowledge of that? Did she strike you, when your pupil, as knowing much about her forbears?"

"Not as much as I did."

"Ah!"

"It is rather an amusing situation, which many college tutors must have encountered from time to time. You have positively to inform a girl that her great-grandfather was prime minister of Great Britain."

"Not quite that, surely."

"Well, no—but at dinner one is allowed a little picturesque exaggeration. Certainly a great-granduncle."

"Did you have to tell Magda just that?"

"Of course not. I'm not aware of any Grinton as having made much mark on the public life of the country. There have been successful city Grintons from time to time, and one or two modest fortunes extorted from the West Indies. But it has been in literature and the arts, and to some extent in philosophy, that oddity has appeared in the family on certain rare occasions."

"Oddity, certainly." Appleby glanced towards Terence Grinton at the foot of the table. "Almost hard to believe. But my wife has told me as much, in a general way. She had oddities in her own family, and there is even some hitchup with a Grinton oddity somewhere in its annals. And Grinton himself mentioned to me earlier today a certain Ambrose Grinton, of whose moral character he seemed not to think highly. Ambrose took up with artists, and collected rubbish from them."

"He also travelled in France and Italy, which Mr. Grinton would certainly consider a dubious activity in itself. I have read a little about Ambrose somewhere, and am not particularly curious about him. But I'd like to know more about Jonathan, Ambrose's grandson, who flourished in the

81

first decades of the eighteenth century. Jonathan collected men of letters—and their productions, no doubt, as well."

"Which is what gives you your interest in him." Appleby said this at a venture, but confidently. It was a fair guess that what Miss Arne had taught Magda Grinton at Somerville had been English literature. The lady was what is known, with a curious ambiguity of language, as an English scholar.

"That is true. Jonathan Grinton belongs to a period in which the relations between writers and artists on the one hand and their patrons among the aristocracy and the gentry on the other was in a curious transitional phase. It is my impression that the writers were a little ahead of the artists and the musicians—and certainly of the actors—in point of social acceptance. But they were scarcely abreast with the French. Voltaire, indeed, could be humiliated and beaten in the street for the mere amusement of a group of nobles. But he belonged to a caste already secure of its rights and regarding itself virtually as an estate of the realm. When he came to England and visited Congreve he was disgusted to find a distinguished dramatist chiefly concerned to cut a figure as a fine gentleman."

Miss Arne, thus showing alarming signs of delivering the proem to a full-scale lecture, paused to address herself to what was probably the last dish of pheasant to appear at Grinton for many months. Appleby being silent and politely attentive, she then went on.

"In the mid-eighteenth century we find Samuel Johnson, the son of an obscure bookseller, received almost everywhere with deep respect. But he handed out the same thing handsomely in return. He believed quite as wholeheartedly as James Boswell did in the grand principle of subordination."

"There had been some awkward chaps rather earlier," Appleby ventured. "Swift, for example."

"Very true. Swift had very little impulse to subordinate himself to any man. And his eventual reward was to hobnob familiarly with a number of distinctly exalted persons. His friend Alexander Pope is another special case. Pope was of course precocious, and was receiving patronage as quite a young man, being entertained in great houses and often writing about them and their owners either agreeably or disagreeably as he felt inclined. If one of his celebrated pieces could be associated with your house or estate, it was quite something."

"Somewhere or other, there's an affair called Pope's Tower."

"At Stanton Harcourt in Oxfordshire. He seems to have been entertained by the Harcourts during 1717 and 1718, when he was working on his translation of the *Iliad*. It was when he was finishing off the fifth volume that there was the tremendous thunderstorm that killed two rural lovers in one another's arms in a harvest field. You will recall the incident, Sir John. The then Lord Harcourt had Pope write an epitaph for them. But that is by the way. We are considering Jonathan Grinton. It was probably some years before the Stanton Harcourt visit that he nobbled the celebrated young poet and lodged him in this house for an unknown but probably quite brief period. If Pope wrote anything about the place it has never been discovered. But it seems not unlikely that he did."

"It was his habit?"

"At *Timon's* Villa let us pass a day, Sir John." Miss Arne quoted this to an effect of mild reproach, as to a pupil inadequately prepared.

"Yes, indeed. Yet hence the *Poor* are cloath'd, the *Hun-*

gry fed." Appleby thus pulled up his socks with admirable speed.

"And of Stanton Harcourt—where he was, I think, very well treated—he left a witty description which has of course survived. It would be pleasant to know a little more about Jonathan. He represents a tiny but not wholly unpromising plot of unexplored territory in eighteenth-century social history."

"I suppose so. But you have never profited by your acquaintance with the family to do a little exploring on your own? On this present visit, for example?"

"Dear me, no!" Miss Arne sounded surprised. "Mr. Grinton, as you can see, would not be well-disposed to anything of the sort. And Mrs. Grinton invites me here from time to time simply as judging it pleasant that her daughter should meet an old teacher. And so it is. Magda is an intelligent girl, and did very well at Somerville." Miss Arne lowered her voice only very slightly. "It is perhaps a pity that she married that intellectually undistinguished young man."

"The auctioneer?"

"I believe that to be his trade, and that he knows the right price for a rare book. A drab accomplishment. He is said to have been at least promisingly freakish as a young man. But some piece of nonsense got him sent down from Oxford, and the endowment hasn't been heard of since."

With this remark—which seemed a trifle freakish in itself—Miss Arne turned and talked briskly to her other neighbour.

Appleby, as well as a very fair dinner, had food for thought before him. What might have appeared a merely freakish suggestion of his own to the effect that undercover literary

84

research had been going on in the Grinton library had received sudden and unexpected reinforcement through this conversation with his learned neighbour. There must be as many scholars who would be delighted to discover such a rarity as an unknown poem by Alexander Pope celebrating or perhaps mocking Grinton and the Grintons. But substantially it would be the pure dry light of scholarship that would be involved. Of course such a minor literary *trouvaille* would have—Appleby supposed— considerable pecuniary value; put up at the right sort of sale, it would be knocked down for quite a comfortable sum. But surely not for anything astronomical. In fact, it seemed unlikely to be for reward of this kind that an elaborate and chancy operation would be mounted. If the solution of the Grinton mystery lay in any such area, enthusiasm rather than cupidity must be the mainspring of the action. And it was extremely unlikely to be enthusiasm of a character prompting the doing of anybody to death.

But all this remained merely perplexing. If one suddenly finds that one has been sufficiently ill-advised to murder somebody, one is quite likely—either immediately or very soon thereafter—to judge it prudent to do something about the body. Drop it down a disused well, or something of that kind. But if one merely comes upon somebody who has died—or who, conceivably, has been inexplicably murdered by somebody else—it is very improbable that any such trafficking with the corpse can have anything to recommend it. One simply hurries off (as Honeybath had done) in search of help.

The circumstances of the moment, however, did not admit of prolonged brooding over the enigma. Miss Arne had presumably finished off with Appleby for the duration of the meal, but the lady on his other hand had been waiting

85

her turn. She was a Mrs. Mustard. So much, and no more, Appleby knew about her. The principal garment encasing her person appeared to be contrived out of a complexity of diaphanous veils, abundantly adequate for decency, the interrelationship of which would have baffled a couturier. Within, she seemed to be of substantial build and mature years. Without, she was further adorned with numerous enormous bangles and two enormous rings. She suggested, if the thought be a conceivable one, a bourgeois version of the late Dame Edith Sitwell. She must be one of Dolly Grinton's queerer fish. So much had Appleby time to observe and conjecture, and then Mrs. Mustard spoke.

"I don't know whether you have heard," she said. "But a most remarkable thing has happened at Grinton this afternoon."

"Indeed?" Appleby took it into his head to speak as one politely expectant before a commonplace remark. "Grinton doesn't strike me as a likely milieu for remarkable happenings."

"Your eyes are sealed." Mrs. Mustard offered this derogatory information with great solemnity. "It is often in the most banal surroundings that we come closest to the heart of the mystery. It is often in lineaments wholly unpurged that we discern the impress of beatitude. Look at Terence Grinton."

Obediently, Appleby looked at Terence Grinton. There was conceivably an elusive sense in which "unpurged" was applicable to what he saw. But this didn't mean that Mrs. Mustard was other than an embarrassing conversationalist. She was going to discourse on New Thought or something of that kind. She probably frequented an ashram and swore by a favourite swami as more certainly in touch with the infinite than any other in the whole swarm of swamis that now raved and recited and maddened round the land. Was it possible to hold her down to earth?

"Here at Grinton, you were saying," Appleby said firmly. "A remarkable happening. Just what?"

"A clear instance of bilocation. Not that bilocation is especially remarkable in itself. In India—I am sure you adore India, Sir John—it is quite common for sacred persons to enjoy the power of instantaneously transporting themselves from one place to another."

"Yes, of course. But now a sacred person has done this here at Grinton, Mrs. Mustard?"

"Not exactly that. And, unfortunately, the higher bilocation appears not to be in question."

"I fear I am terribly ignorant. There are two sorts of bilocation?"

"Certainly—but in a subtle relationship the one with the other. Common bilocation is a matter of being, say, in London at one moment and removed to New York the next. In the higher bilocation a person is in two distinct places—Paris and Peking, it may be—simultaneously."

"And at Grinton we have been favoured only with the lower variety, which is quite a humdrum affair?"

"Well, yes—but with one *very* important difference. Surely you have been told about it?" For an instant Mrs. Mustard glanced almost suspiciously at Appleby.

"Well, yes. I have heard a rumour. But do tell."

"The person in this instance is said to have been *dead*." Mrs. Mustard paused impressively. "I don't think I ever heard of such a thing before. It is of the highest theoretical significance, since there can be no volition on the part of a corpse. It might have been acted upon by some exterior agency. You do agree?"

"Oh, I don't see that, Mrs. Mustard. We know devilish

little about that sort of thing, after all. That's where the fun lies, wouldn't you say? And a corpse may have a trick or two left to it in a surprising way. Take a chicken now. It's said you can chop its head off and it will still run clean round the fowl yard. And there are all those ghosts— veridical phantasms of the dead, I ought to say—strayed from the scaffold with their own heads under their arms. Prima facie, I don't see that the dead must be denied the pleasures of bilocation. But about this current affair. Does it mean that at Grinton we now have two identical dead bodies instead of just one? The police must feel anything of the sort as decidedly an *embarras de richesse*. But I'm being stupid, of course. You must forgive me. It's an unfamiliar terrain to me, you know. Two identical bodies could result only from the higher bilocation, and this is just the bread-and-butter lower one. A dead body found in one place is later discovered mysteriously transported to another place."

"*Mysteriously*—yes."

"Then we are in perfect agreement, after all," Appleby said, and applied himself to what—rather disconcertingly—bore a distinct relationship to Welsh rabbit.

8

CHARLES HONEYBATH HAD FOUND HIMSELF BETWEEN
Judith Appleby and Terence Grinton's married daughter,
Magda Tancock. He began by taking a cautious look at the
younger woman. Although she had two children in their
early teens, she was far from consenting to look matronly.
That bandbox look (Honeybath told himself) belonged to
the kind of young woman who gives much thought to the
figure she is going to cut at her next party. It is not a
disposition or preoccupation to be regarded in a particularly unsympathetic light—or not by a painter. Transferring
that sort of high finish to a canvas without turning choco-
late-box artist or society photographer presented problems
of considerable interest in themselves. At the same time,
Honeybath was quite glad that it was to Magda's father and
not to Magda herself that he was soon to be devoting his
professional energies.

Or was he? Might it not be possible that the afternoon's
obscure events would develop in some fashion so macabre
or sinister as to preclude for a time his going forward with
his commission in that sort of decent calm it required? This
was a self-centred and even slightly morbid thought, and
the immediate remedy was to start talking to Judith, and

defer encounter with the less familiar lady. This he now managed to do. What he didn't manage was to advance a topic unconnected with the sensational events of the day.

"Judith," he asked, "have you heard that the police have cleared out? I ran into that fellow Denver in the hall, and he actually shook hands with me in a valedictory fashion. He might have been a specialist who had been peering into my inside, and was just off to do the same thing by another patient. But he'd think about my case, and send his opinion to my G.P. It positively made me feel on a danger list—that in no time I'd be in intensive care in the local police station."

"My dear Charles, what a fantastic idea! Or are you merely being good fun?"

"Well, one must try, you know, to make a moment merry. But there really is something slightly unnerving in not being quite believed. John, God bless him, is a believer. He believes not only that I came on a man in the library, but that I came on a dead man. Denver credits me with coming on *something*—or I rather think he does. But I seem to sense a general persuasion that poor old Honeybath was simply seeing things. His job, of course. Even portrait painters make their living ninety percent out of portraying what isn't there. Every year the walls of Burlington House proclaim it."

"Thank goodness, Charles, you keep so entirely cheerful."

"I'm not cheerful."

"Gamesome, then, and willing to entertain. And I can see the situation *is* vexatious. But not that there's anything to complain about in the police having taken themselves off."

"It's tantamount to saying that *nothing* has happened."

"I can't see that. They probably have a rule about an eight-hour day, and getting home to the wife and kiddies. They'll turn up again in the morning, and fall to with a will, arresting us left and right. This company will never sit down to dinner together again."

"It's a mixed lot, isn't it? Fourteen all told, if I've counted right, and several of them I still don't know from Adam. Who's that extraordinary woman on John's left?"

"A Mrs. Mustard. She was talking to me before dinner, and it seems she's entirely ready to take over from Mr. Denver."

"Good Lord! A kind of Miss Marple—female sleuth?"

"No, nothing so prosaic. She thinks we ought to call spirits from the vasty deep. Discover the truth by holding some sort of séance, in fact. It seems that she herself possesses quite outstanding mediumistic powers."

"Heaven save us!" Honeybath sounded quite genuinely alarmed. "But at least the woman on John's other side isn't off her head. A Miss or Doctor or Professor Arne. I had some talk with her this morning. Agreeable and well-informed—in the right proportions, too."

Judith took a moment to consider this last discriminating remark.

"One can certainly have too much," she then said, "either of the quality on the one hand or of the acquirement on the other. I hope you're not going to find my remote kinsman Terence extremely boring. He comes more short on the second than on the first, and even his agreeableness is a bit chancy."

"He seems to have the power of being absolutely intolerable without occasioning much resentment. I have to come to understand him, you know, and I'm not going to find it easy. Do you think that he's perhaps one of the celebrated Grinton odd bods heavily disguised?"

"Whether he is or isn't, Charles, you ought to paint him as just that. It would be a stimulating exercise."

"No doubt I need stimulating badly, Judith. But if I do paint him—which I begin to doubt—I'll paint him straight."

"Portrait of a gentleman thinking about the chicken fund."

"Whatever's that?"

"Something to do with the hunt. Terence spends a lot of time brooding over it. He thinks he ought to have control of the chicken fund. But it seems not to have been the customary thing with the Nether Barset. Do you know that there are seventeenth-century poems with titles like 'Instructions to a Painter,' and beginning 'Paint me this' or 'Paint me that'? Paint me Terence as a Napoleon of high finance. Get it all into the furrow on his brow." Judith glanced briefly at Honeybath and judged that this chatter had sufficiently relieved his mind. "And now you'd better talk to Magda," she said.

So Honeybath prepared to address himself to this task. He had a few moments' leisure to do so, since Magda was engaged with her other neighbour, an elderly red-faced man very much in the Terence tradition. Apart from Miss Arne's commendation of Magda as a capable pupil, Honeybath knew very little about the Tancocks. Was Magda the Grintons' only child? If so—and Honeybath had heard nothing of a son—the young gentleman who, with his parents and sister, had gone in pursuit of rabbits that afternoon was presumably heir to the Grinton estate and fortune, such as it was. Perhaps he would be required to take on a hyphenated life as Mr. Tancock-Grinton or Grinton-Tancock. His mother could scarcely be asked about this, but it would be in order to express civil interest in the children. Then there was Giles Tancock's profession. Apparently it involved standing on a rostrum and banging some convenient surface with a gavel. What thereupon changed hands was commonly no doubt an object of refined interest in one or another field of art of bibliopoly. Nevertheless it was hard (at least for Charles Honeybath, many of whose notions came out of Noah's ark) to view the activity as quite properly that of a gentleman. Certainly to say to Magda, "I gather your husband's an auctioneer?" would probably be regarded as a little lacking in the felicitious. "Are you a Londoner, as I am?" might be a bit better. But in rural society (from which Magda herself sprang) "Londoner" was often much the same in implication as "townee" or even "weekender." Semantically—Honeybath reflected—"weekender" was interesting. A couple of generations ago, most persons of consequence were weekenders more weekends than not: moving augustly round one another's country residences. No doubt that activity continued, if on a diminished scale. But more commonly a weekender was now a citizen who had bought a village hovel, gentrified it, and when in residence knew nothing of his neighbours or even of their dogs and cats.

"Did the children enjoy their afternoon with the rabbits?" Honeybath asked. The red-faced man had fallen silent.

"Not in the least. It's a ritual activity insisted upon by my father when we pay one of these family visits to Grinton.

Demetrius and Florinda aren't in the least enchanted by it."

"Children are not always very receptive of the pleasures prepared for them." Honeybath, who knew little about children, supposed this to have a reasonable chance of being true. Give your progeny affected names like Demetrius and Florinda, he was reflecting, and you can't expect them to be keen on the simpler country pleasures.

"My husband sets them a very bad example—simply slinking away and going after his own affairs. Of course it *is* rather disgusting. There is a nasty old man with two or three ferrets in a bag—and the poor things haven't even the chance of a square meal, since their snouts are tied up before the fun begins. Otherwise, it seems, they would simply settle down to a long guzzle and a quiet snooze inside the warren. As it is, out come the rabbits, and Demetrius is supposed to shoot them dead. Of course all he has is a little air gun, and he hasn't bagged a rabbit yet. But I am always afraid he may bag Florinda."

"That must be a considerable anxiety."

"It's not as if it's the poor boy's duty to instruct himself in such rusticities. He isn't going to have Grinton, you know."

Honeybath felt that "I'm sorry to hear it," would be an excessive response to this information, which was both mildly surprising as being volunteered in this way and such as entirely to confound his own idle speculations of only a few minutes before. So he only said, "Is that so?" much as if he had been given information on the present state of the Grinton tennis court.

"I have an elder brother who does some sort of farming in South Africa because he doesn't get on with my father, but who will arrive and take over when the time comes. It's not something we at all resent, Giles and I. Florinda is

94

going to do ballet—though I say it she's a most talented child—and it would be marvellous if Demetrius did too. We've been assured by somebody who really knows that he has just the right legs. There's a lot of silly prejudice about male dancers, don't you think? About their sexual habits, and the idea that their job is simply to take a deep breath and hold the women up in the air with a palm of the hand to their bottom. So I'd *adore* Demetrius, as I say, to become a ballet dancer too. Wouldn't it be wonderful if he turned out like Nureyev, or even Nijinsky himself, and Florinda were as good as the Fonteyn? A *prima ballerina assoluta!* A stunning *pas de deux* by a brother and sister would be quite something at Covent Garden."

"I shall hope to see their debut," Honeybath said dishonestly. Mrs. Tancock's speech had depressed him a good deal—the lady not being all that might be expected of an approved Somerville girl privileged to have been taught by Miss Kate Arne. Silly metropolitan ways, he said to himself, and society is turning wholly rubbishing. Aloud, he asked a relevant question. "When does a dancer's full-time education begin, Mrs. Tancock? At humbler levels of the same sort of thing—for circuses, and so forth—the infant puts in most of his time being taught to tumble right from the start." It was perhaps not quite innocently that Honeybath produced this demeaning comparison. "Will Demetrius have to go to a special sort of school almost straight away?"

"Dear me, no. Naturally, he must go through Eton first. And Florinda will at least begin at a proper girl's public school—although certainly one at which a great deal of attention is given to dancing. It's all going to be dreadfully expensive. Of course we hope—or at least Giles hopes— that my father will put his hand in his pocket. Giles says he wouldn't come within a mile of Grinton if it wasn't for that. I have doubts about it myself. For one thing, I'm not sure my father has a pocket to put a hand in. And I suspect that, really and truly, Giles thinks the same. I've heard him say you can tell by the claret."

Honeybath found himself putting down his own claret glass abruptly, as if to avoid the enormity of appearing to be checking up on this last aspersion. He had listened in deepening dumbfounderment to Magda Tancock's entire performance, and could only suppose that devastating candour had become the "in" entertainment at such social gatherings as she normally frequented. Or perhaps it was a turn her set put on when constrained to converse with boring old persons such as Royal Academicians and emeritus professors and the higher clergy. And suddenly Magda Tancock said a surprising thing.

"I've been talking absolutely out of turn, Mr. Honeybath, and nineteen to the dozen. Anything rather than get on to what you found in that library."

"My dear lady, it wouldn't occur to me to broach the subject. It had much better be let sleep for a time. If possible, put clean out of mind."

"I find myself thinking about it a good deal. A mysterious death in the house, and policemen asking everybody questions. I suppose it's silly to feel it rather frightening. But I do." Magda paused for a moment. "The claret seems all right to me," she said. And she was then almost silent for the rest of the meal.

After the claret there was a sip of port, and then Dolly Grinton gathered up the ladies and departed to the drawing room. The gentlemen shuffled down the table towards their host, before whom Burrow, with an air of subdued prodigality, set down a fresh decanter. Those less familiar with the habits of the house waited hopefully for the appearance of cigars, but Burrow had concluded his ministrations and now disappeared—perhaps to a refection of cold pheasant and claret in his pantry.

Terence Grinton picked up the fresh decanter, and almost forgot to go through the ritual of replenishing the glass of the man to his right before applying himself liberally to the stuff on his own behalf. It was clear that he felt some formal remarks to be incumbent upon him, but that he wasn't at all clear what they were. There was a situation requiring thought—that most vexatious and slippery of commodities. He cleared his throat—nervously, yet so explosively that it might be supposed he had found one of his numerous occasions for inordinate mirth.

"Terribly sorry," he said gruffly, "about all that bother earlier this evening. Owe an apology to you fellows. All blown over, of course. Nothing in it at all. Silly that we sent for that policeman. Idea was to reassure the women."

These clipped utterances were received in silence, except that one anxiously tactful guest muttered a supportive "Quite right," and then nervously lit a cigarette. Terence would no doubt have done well to turn to a topic more likely to conduce to relaxed general chat. But he seemed to feel that the mystery of the library must be expanded upon.

"We must all sympathize with Honeybath," he said. "Indeed, I owe him an apology. Honeybath, my dear fellow, I apologize. Everybody knows that somehow or other nobody happens ever to go into the library. Just one of those things. So when Honeybath went in—a perfectly natural thing to do, of course, particularly if one is of an enquiring mind—he was naturally rather put out at finding another fellow in the room. Various misunderstandings followed, but have all been cleared up. We can put it out of our heads. By the way, I believe Dolly is thinking of bridge. But if anybody is inclined to billiards, I'm his man. And she won't mind at all."

Honeybath—although only minutes earlier he had been recommending the "out of mind" procedure to Magda Tancock—was naturally not gratified by this performance. He was, in fact, outraged—and the more so because no clear course of action was apparent to him. Apart from a slight imputation of vulgar curiosity (not unjustified, for that matter), he hadn't been directly aspersed by his host of any unbecoming behaviour. It hadn't been suggested that he had shuffled or told fibs or got in a funk, so he couldn't at once rise and withdraw alike from his commission and the entire Grinton demesne. And it was Terence Grinton—the old fool—who for some reason was in a funk. He had (Honeybath felt sure) a bad conscience about the whole thing, and just couldn't leave it alone. This was why, quite out of the blue, he had made a speech the only intelligible content of which was to effect that nobody must be cross with Charles Honeybath R.A., who was only a harmless dotard with an unfortunate tendency to hallucinations. Grinton had even put a charitable interpretation on the thing by subscribing to the fiction that there had been "another fellow in the room." Or so Honeybath interpreted those rambling remarks.

"Silly old bastard." This was murmured into Honeybath's ear, apparently by way of moral support, by a familiar voice proving to be that of Hallam Hillam. But Honeybath, although thoroughly disposed to concur in the sentiment, disapproved of its enunciation. One really ought not to say that sort of thing about a man, however tiresome, whose port one was at that moment drinking. Or certainly it shouldn't be thus murmured by a virtual stranger. From Appleby it would have been entirely comforting. Honeybath resolved to seek out Appleby as soon as they got back to the drawing room.

"It's a very trying thing," he said with reserve, "for a man to find happening in his house. So one mustn't be censorious."

"There's been a happening, all right," Hillam went on—undeterred and in a louder voice. "So it's absurd to think to huff and puff it away. And I don't like it. It worries me. It upsets things."

"It is very generally upsetting, of course." Honeybath was conscious of feeling puzzled. It was almost as if this man Hillam was angry as well as at a loss before the mystery, and had spoken in an unguarded way. "Have you ever taken a glance into that library yourself?"

Honeybath had asked this question quite thoughtlessly: simply because a further word or two seemed necessary before shaking the fellow off. But Hillam was disconcerted by it, much as if it had been the pouncing kind of thing that Inspector Denver might have fired off at him.

"I don't know Grinton at all well," Hillam said. "This is my first visit here. Mrs. G. was very keen I should come down."

This was scarcely an answer. It was in fact evasive. So Honeybath concluded that Hillam was another who, in the last couple of days, had taken a peep at the confounded room, but without any such disconcerting experience as had attended his own indiscretion. And now Hillam was well established in the chair next to him; no general talk was getting under way; it seemed necessary to continue some sort of tête-à-tête.

"I gather"—Honeybath said by way of at least changing

the subject—"that Indian antiquities are your particular thing: a field I'm sadly ignorant of."

"Well, not exactly." Hillam hesitated oddly: it was almost as if he would have been glad to claim that this was indeed so. "I suppose I ought to be called an art historian."

This was awkward. The man *was*, in some way, persistently awkward. But the present awkwardness was intelligible. Honeybath must at least in a general way know his way about among art historians. So not already knowing that this curating Hallam Hillam was among them rendered a slightly injurious effect. Of course this was a common liability when moving around in learned and academic circles. The crude way of dealing with the thing was to ejaculate something like, "What, *the* Hillam!" and hope for the best. But Charles Honeybath wasn't good at dealing in such parlour subterfuges. So he was relieved that at this point Terence Grinton got reluctantly to his feet and suggested joining the ladies. Honeybath, however, joined Appleby—winking him (it might be said) into a corner of the drawing room.

"John," he said, "I wonder if you can advise me? It seems to me, you know, that I find myself in rather an awkward position."

"I'm sorry to hear it." Appleby reflected that Charles was rather prone to finding himself—or perhaps feeling himself—to be in an awkward position. Although a person both of philosophical mind and very adequate social aplomb, he exposed to the world a considerable area of vulnerability in all things connected with his art.

"It's this fellow Grinton," Honeybath said. "I'm here on a purely professional engagement, and know next to nothing about him. Whereas you are an old family friend, as I

100

understand the matter. So of course I hesitate to say anything disparaging about him."

"My dear Charles, 'old family friend' is inaccurate. He's not even an old family friend of Judith's: just a distant relation she feels ought to be given a nod to from time to time. It's one of those tedious upper-class things."

"Well, yes." Honeybath nodded understandingly. Although, as a boy, chance had taken him to Eton, it no more occurred to him that he belonged to an upper class than that he belonged to an aristocracy. He was just a painter. "But what troubles me, you see, is what he said or implied about me at his wife's dinner table. He told the company at large—wouldn't you agree?—that I am virtually a loony."

"It was perhaps a little lacking in address. But the man is clearly uneasy for some reason about this whole affair, and says anything that comes into his not exactly thin head. If it really bothers you, you might yourself be charged with owning a thin skin. Forget it."

"Yes. But it's the business, you see, of my being commissioned to take the chap's likeness. Ought I, in the circumstances, to pocket the money of his subscribers—ingenuous souls, I imagine, just like himself? He can't very well get out of it when a thing like that has been fixed up. But he may very reasonably resent having to sit to a man he has decided sees things. That's how he'd put it. So I might see heaven knows what in *him*."

"Why not? It's your job. And it's as near to objective fact as makes no matter that you did veritably see something. Precisely what, may be not quite certain. But that's no matter. There *is* a mystery, I assure you. And you happened to be the first to stumble on it."

"What about the police? They seem simply to have

101

cleared out. Washed their hands discreetly of the whole load of rubbish—which of course is how Grinton judges it."

"Charles, I doubt whether he does anything of the kind. And certainly the police don't. I've thought about it a lot, and it's my opinion that our friend Denver is up to something."

Honeybath was silent for a moment. He was clearly impressed and a little disposed to be comforted.

"You mean, John, that Denver has some sort of clue?"

"That I don't know at all. But I have. It's in the pocket of my dinner jacket at this moment."

"My dear Holmes, you amaze me!" Honeybath was sufficiently heartened to decline upon this piece of ancient facetiousness.

"Something very little remarkable in itself, but remarkably so as having turned up decidedly in the wrong place." Appleby loyally preserved an oracular note. "You remember my dodging down into the library's cellarage? Absolute chaos, and I was in it no time at all. One might expect to find almost anything. But not what I did find."

"Which was?"

"A copy of a quite recent bookseller's catalogue. To be precise, *Blackwell's Rare Books: Catalogue A27*. It's called 'Antiquarian Books on Travel & Topography.' Here it is. Look at it. Item 269, where someone had made a pencil mark in the margin. Read it right through. It's a model of exact bibliographical record."

So Honeybath—with an occasional wary glance at the rest of the company—read it.

269 **Shaw** (Rev. Stebbing) The History and Antiquities of Staffordshire. Compiled from the Manuscripts of Huntback, Loxdale, Bishop Lyttelton, and other Collections

102

of Dr. Wilkes, the Rev. T. Feilde &c. Including Erd-
wick's Survey of the County, and Approved Parts of
Dr. Plot's Natural History. The Whole brought down
to the Present Time, interspersed with Pedigrees and
Anecdotes of Families; Observations on Agriculture,
Commerce, Mines and Manufactories, and Illustrated
with a very full and correct New Map of the County.
Agri Staffordiensis Icon, and many other Plates and
Tables. 2 vols. *Printed by and for J. Nichols, 1798–*
1801, LARGE PAPER *(?), with 82 plates, 2 large folding*
maps, and some 32 illustrations printed in the text, in
both the full-page and smaller illustrations extensive
use has been made of the aquatint process, as well as
the usual copper engraving, the pagination is erratic
throughout, folio, *contemporary paper boards, some-*
what rubbed and worn, paper backstrips repaired, all
edges uncut, contained in two solander cases, in brown
cloth, size 20 ins x 12 ins. (Upcott 1176)   **£650.00**

"And 270," Appleby said, "is more or less the same work,
and is marked with a pencil too. It would cost you a hundred pounds less."

"I see." In fact, Honeybath didn't see at all. "What's a
solander case?"

"I believe it's a box made in the form of a book: a kind of
little brother to that dummy door. But you see the point;
why, I mean, this catalogue can be called a clue. Clearly it
was left behind fairly recently by somebody rummaging
down there. So it ties in—or to some extent it ties in—with
a notion I sketched out for you at the start. Clandestine
investigation of the riches, or supposed riches, of the Grinton library. But not quite the sort of investigation I had in
mind. The academic pernoctationist, you remember, avid
for the advancement of learning. This isn't Staffordshire,

103

and nobody is likely to be prompted to ransack Grinton specifically in search of Staffordshire antiquities for their own sake. I see this chap as having had half a dozen or more catalogues of this sort, and ticking off in them any particularly costly items that he came upon here. Or that general idea. There are lots of possibilities. For example, he gradually gets together a pile of such things—a cache of them, you may say—and proposes to remove them *en bloc* on some favourable occasion. Anyway, a money-making rather than a knowledge-making ploy. In fact, a straight criminal enterprise, probably on a fairly small scale, but conceivably on a moderately large one. It's interesting. As such, it lends a little support to the conjecture that one kind of crime led—through some untimely discovery, or the like—to a much graver one. But I'd need a good deal of stronger evidence before I put my own money on that."

"There's stuff in this description"—and Honeybath tapped the catalogue—"on aquatints and copper engraving." It had come into Honeybath's head that he had perhaps something to contribute to this impressive detective process. He glanced once more cautiously round the drawing room. "Might a special interest in these arts be involved? I ask because I've discovered something about that chap Hillam—whom for some reason I rather distrust. Indian religions and so on are his hobby. But he told me in the dining room that by profession he's an art historian."

"More specifically, an iconographer, according to Dolly."

"Is that so? I suppose one ought to have heard of him. But, John, there was another thing. I thought I detected him as being a little put out when I happened to ask him whether he had ever had a look round the library here."

"Well, well! Any further revelations, Charles?"

"I'm afraid not." But even as Honeybath shook his head, his expression altered. "Good heavens!" he exclaimed. "It has come back to me—just as you said it would. About the dead man's clothes. And his shoes as well! I habitually notice such things when male sitters turn up in my studio. Savile Row, or off the peg. A kind of *Tailor and Cutter* interest." Honeybath was almost incoherent before the magnitude of his discovery. "The corpse's togs. American."

Appleby received this excited communication with respect.

"Bravo!" he said. "The plot thickens."

9

WHEN APPLEBY WENT UP TO HIS ROOM IT WAS TO FIND HIS wife already in bed, and reading.

"I've borrowed a book from Burrow," she said. "Burrow for a good borrow."

"Whoever is Burrow?"

"Burrow is Terence's butler. You ought to talk to him. He's an interesting man."

"So is Terence, in a fashion—or so I've come to believe." Appleby began to undress. "What sort of book does one borrow from Burrow?"

"I'll give you a guess, and a hint. It's historical."

"Butlers—a dying race—lead sheltered lives until they fade away. So they like reading rough stuff. It's a history of pugilism."

"Wrong. It's called *Reliquiae Grintonianae*."

"Impossible."

"Not at all. It's an anecdotal affair, apparently privately printed, and brought together by one Simon Upcott, a cleric of antiquarian tastes, who was Vicar of Grinton Parva early in the eighteenth century. And, of course, it's all about the Grintons."

"Well, I'm blessed!" Appleby was in his pyjamas. "How does this Burrow come by such a thing?"

"Burrow is an antiquarian too. His father was butler here before him. So he's more interested in the Grintons than the Grintons are."

"That may well be. What have I done with my toothbrush?"

"It's in front of your nose, John. Or your teeth."

"So it is. Has Burrow filched this book from that wretched library?"

"Not at all. He has his own collection, ranged on long shelves in his pantry. In a house like this one ought always to have a chat with the butler in his pantry. It's considered quite proper. But not with a housemaid in a linen room."

"I'll remember that as a warning. Have you come on anything by or about Jonathan Grinton, who patronized Pope?"

"No, not yet—and I don't know that the book gets as far as that. There's a lot about Thomas Sackville Grinton, whose father married into the nobility, and who was a top scholar in his time. And about Ambrose, a Restoration eccentric. Ambrose went in for travel, and what would later have been called Bohemian society."

"Really, Judith, I'm coming to hear too much about the Grinton odd bods—all remorselessly marching towards poor Charles and his wretched corpse and the cockeyed theory hovering in my head about it. I'd like to hear about the quiet and ordinary Grintons: generations and generations of them, all leading up to Terence."

"I don't think I'd call Terence quiet."

"Perhaps not. Did you get a hint from someone to chum up with this elderly Ganymede?"

"Burrow? Yes, from Dolly. I got her on to her husband's family. She said she had never been told much about it, or bothered to read it up. Nor have the Grintons themselves.

Their attitude in the matter is a little like that of Count Philippe Auguste Mathias de Villiers de L'Isle-Adam's Axel towards the mere business of living."

"Judith, for heaven's sake!"

"Axel is made to say that our servants will do that for us. At Grinton it's apparently servants who hold the position of historiographers-royal."

"You're saying all this because you don't want me to mess around with this stupid mystery."

"Well, it does seem to me a family affair, and likely to lead to a good deal of embarrassment."

"A family affair is certainly an element in it. I wouldn't go further than that. But I can't be certain the missing man wasn't murdered. And that's a serious thing. If anything comes into my mind that might be useful to Denver and his crowd it's my duty to pursue it."

"It's your ingrained habit, you mean. I can't take you anywhere without your indulging a trick of the old rage."

"Judith, you're up to something of the sort yourself, with these molelike researches in that ridiculous *Reliquiae Grintonianae.*"

"True enough." Judith Appleby was seldom very serious in these attempts to dissuade her husband from detective activities. "Would you like to have a read of the thing now?"

"I'll have a look at it in the morning," Appleby said with a certain dignity. "At the moment, I propose to go to sleep."

But this was not to be. Appleby lay awake for some time, obstinately thinking his way through the Grinton enigma. The last piece of hard evidence to have turned up was Charles Honeybath's sudden memory about the dead man's clothes. It is commonly women that notice such matters. But Charles spent much of his working life reproduc-

108

ing on canvas gents' suitings of one sort of another, and was thus obliged to cultivate what might be called the sartorial eye. What Appleby had similarly been obliged to cultivate was alertness to every sort of criminal ingenuity. In the world of Scotland Yard—so largely a dream world—it was necessary to think twice about a corpse in American clothes—and shoes. The corpse might have been stripped of honest English garments and shoved into those alien ones in the interest of some deep and devilish design. In a really high-class detective story it would almost necessarily be so; the reader would feel cheated if it turned out otherwise. But—Appleby firmly decided—here at Grinton had been an honest-to-god American interloper now dead—or dead except in the wholesomely sceptical mind of Inspector Denver.

So far, so good—and to Charles a very high mark, indeed. Like the poet among hedgehogs, he was a man who noticed such things. He had noticed something dusty about the man, and also the bizarre circumstance that he had a cobweb in his hair. About the first of these further facts there was nothing remarkable, since the library wasn't a particularly well-dusted room. But the cobweb was another matter. Unless—a morbid thought—a spider had got rapidly to work on the corpse with the benevolent intention of weaving it a shroud, it powerfully suggested that fairly soon before his death the man had been occupied in the library's cellarage, which Appleby had himself discovered to be dusty and cobwebby in a big way. But this wasn't all. Honeybath had noticed something else.

Appleby almost sat up in bed as he realized the shock which this face was suddenly occasioning in him. Why ever hadn't he pondered it before?

Malign glee . . . a malicious grin . . . enjoying a nasty

joke . . . This sequence of words from Honeybath was now sounding in Appleby's ear again, and he realized with astonishment that it had evoked from him no more than a feeble joke of his own and an obscure medical term. Rictus. There was such a word, but he would need a dictionary to tell him exactly what it meant. Whereas there was something uncommonly exact, or at least vivid, in the image Honeybath had called up. Moreover, when studying a human face Charles Honeybath must own professional expertise in a very high degree.

Appleby, thus alert in darkness, perversely asked himself whether he was half asleep. How could there be any significance in this vagary of physiology? At the moment of death or just after it, random twitchings no doubt occur all over the body, and it may well be that the features fall into some chance configuration which it is idle to think of reading in any meaningful sense. Was anything more to be said about Charles's impression than this? Surely not. Yet Appleby felt that he had somewhere read a recondite study of the matter which had advanced more complex considerations. Many living men carry around in their cast of countenance a silent exhibition of their cast of mind. One goes about looking supercilious, another severe, yet another furtive or alarmed. Sometimes the effect remains after death; sometimes it is, as it were, neutralised or swailed away, so that what is left may be seen either as a nothingness or a noble calm. Into some interpretations of the thing imaginative or sentimental or pietistic fancies intrude: the dying man has glimpsed before him heavenly joys or the flames of hell.

This was sombre territory—and suddenly Appleby found himself confronting something macabre. It was the story of

110

a wake, a vigil maintained beside the body of a man eminent as a philosopher or a dramatist—Schopenhauer, Strindberg?—of strongly pessimistic persuasion. The features of this man had settled into an unaccustomed expression of calm nobility. Then suddenly in the silence of the night a small strange clatter was heard, and the dead face was found contorted in a ferocious snarl. It was because some odd chemistry had operated and the dead man's false teeth had tumbled out of his mouth.

The story was probably apocryphal, Appleby told himself; it might even have been invented by one of his own sons who went in for modishly improbable fictions. Nor was it very relevant to Charles Honeybath's experience. What Charles had seen, or believed he saw, was a man instantaneously struck dead while momentarily under the influence of a pleasurable malice. Under what sort of conditions might one find that? Perhaps under the conditions of warfare. A bullet finding a man in the act of successfully raining bullets into others; blown up in the act of launching a torpedo.

These were ugly reflections and speculations; and there was no point in them. Such things didn't happen at Grinton. Appleby had just told himself this when he sat up in bed very abruptly indeed. Faintly but unmistakably, the sound of a pistol shot had made itself heard in the house.

Judith slept on undisturbed—nor did anybody seem to have been awakened in the immediately adjoining bedrooms. Appleby got out of bed and opened the door. A long corridor lay in darkness, but there was a glimmer of light at the end of it. Listening intently, Appleby thought he heard voices—one of them an angry voice—in a distant quarter of the house. He slipped on a dressing gown and slippers and fished an electric torch out of his suitcase. Burglars with an adequate presence of mind sometimes found and flicked off a master switch, thus securing a convenient darkness holding up identification or pursuit. Then he hurried down the corridor.

It was the main staircase of the house that was lit up in a subdued way: probably a normal disposition of things at night. Stepped one below another, like advertisements on an Underground escalator, there hung a succession of Victorian oil paintings of fox-hunting life. They bore titles, he recalled, like *Squire Grinton with the Nether Barset Hunt* and *Melton Mowbray: A Strong Scent* and *Returning Home after a Good Day.* Like the tiny John Varley in the drawing room, they wouldn't fetch much under the hammer. But there were plenty of objects at Grinton worth making off with, although probably taken very little account of by their proprietor. Grintons had been a home-keeping crowd on the whole. But such of them as had wandered abroad—the scandalous Ambrose, for example—had probably been men of sufficient enterprise to possess themselves of objects of artistic or antiquarian interest as they moved. Thus among those commonplace busts skyed in the library there might well be something authentically Hellenic brought unobtrusively home in the baggage of such a traveller.

Appleby reached the ground floor, and the voices were immediately louder. It was, in fact, from the library that they came. The burglary, if burglary it was, didn't own the nature of a chance distraction. It wasn't an irrelevance. Almost certainly, it tied in with what Appleby was coming to think of as the absurdity, the zany mystery of the missing corpse.

The library door was open; a single low light was on; and the notoriously unfrequented room had become bewilderingly the setting of a nocturnal levee. Mrs. Mustard certainly seemed to have just got out of bed; she might have been described as clothed in white samite, mystic, wonderful; from a capacious woollen handbag which she carried there protruded what appeared to be a planchette and a tambourine. What she was doing here at this unholy hour defied speculation. Inspector Denver and two uniformed constables did not. It came to Appleby that he might almost have expected them. In a corner of his mind there must have lodged the knowledge that the obtrusive departure of the police from Grinton had been a thoroughly bogus affair; that the wily Denver had in fact been baiting a trap. In addition to the spiritually minded Mrs. Mustard, what the trap had caught was Terence Grinton (not that Terence hadn't a perfect right to visit at any hour this imposing part of his property), Giles Tancock, and Hallam Hillam.

Terence held the centre of the stage. He also held a revolver—and this was plainly the weapon the discharge of which had broken in upon Appleby's detective cogitations. But it didn't look as if the outraged householder had positively been trying to murder—or even wing—another of the participants in the gathering. He seemed rather to have discharged the weapon warningly and wrathfully in air. There was a scattering of gilded plasterwork on the floor. And just beneath a cornice, blind but many-minded Homer had ceased to preside over the scene. Homer, at least, had been no Hellenic marble, but plaster too. Only the neck and shoulders were left of him.

***

Faced by this unexpected congregation, Appleby found it to be Denver's processes of mind that were easiest to come by. Denver had tumbled to the fact (which, after all, was fairly obvious) that the locale of the Grinton mystery was its point of cardinal significance. Things hadn't just happened to happen in the library; they had happened *because* of the library. This was certain. But as well as a certainty there was something that could be guessed at. The solitude of the library was seldom intruded upon. One of the Grintons' guests, the artist Mr. Honeybath, had chanced so to intrude. He had come upon something distinctly unexpected, had hastened to seek help, and within a very short time had returned along with Sir John Appleby. These two men had in turn and together come upon another unexpected setup; and at that point it might be said that investigation had begun. This sequence of events carried at least a suggestion of *interruption.* Honeybath, in fact, had conceivably broken in upon an unfinished activity. For somebody or other something in the library remained unachieved—perhaps simply unlocated. Appear to abandon the library; leave it, so to speak, to its own devices. The interested and interrupted party might seek an early opportunity to return.

This, Appleby felt, had been good if rather speculative thinking. And it had borne fruit. Only what Denver and his nocturnal ambush had emerged upon had been an unexpected cloud of witnesses. Denver was clearly at something of a loss, but at this moment he was putting a bold face on the matter.

"And will you please tell me," he was saying to Terence Grinton, "how you came to be discharging a firearm in this room in the middle of the night?"

114

"Why the devil should I?" This came from Grinton at his maximum bellow, and he bore every appearance of being minded to discharge the firearm all over again. "It's my own room in my own house, isn't it, confound you?" It was detectably in considerable confusion of mind that Grinton advanced this blustering argument. He was both bewildered and scared: there could be no doubt of that. "And what are you doing here, anyway? Didn't we tell you to go away, and take those fellows along with you? Do you consider yourself entitled to burgle the place simply because you have an escort of a couple of coppers? Who has issued a warrant entitling you to behave in this way? Name the magistrate, and show me what he has signed to. I'll have your Chief Constable know about your conduct."

This speech, it seemed to Appleby, contrived to be at once imbecile and formidable. In a sense, the owner of Grinton undeniably had the law on his side. But it only meant that the man had to be brought to a better mind. Appleby spoke.

"Grinton," he said peaceably, "I hope I don't intrude, or speak out of turn. But I must point out that when a firearm is discharged there is always a possibility that the act has been intended to endanger human life. Until that has been cleared up, the fact that you are on your own ground is totally irrelevant. Do calm down, and try to understand that."

Grinton's response to this was surprisingly sensible. He gave a brisk kick at the plaster debris at his feet, and simultaneously pointed upwards at the demolished bust of the author of the *Iliad.* "I fired the thing," he bellowed, "only to scare the lights out of that blasted woman." And now he pointed at Mrs. Mustard. "One of my wife's crackpot crowd, behaving like an imbecile while all sane people are in bed."

This was scarcely a courteous manner of describing a guest, but the lady herself seemed scarcely offended by it. She bore a solemn and rapt expression, like one who has become adept—Appleby thought—at attaining a state of Stodge or the Higher Indifference. And the impression of a remove from common mortals was not enhanced by Mrs. Mustard's raising a hand in air and inscribing on it with an index finger a complex if invisible hieroglyphic of what could only be the deepest mystic significance.

"Spirits," Mrs. Mustard said, "walk abroad at night."

This, after so impressive a leadup, came as an almost banal remark, and for a moment nobody had any comment to offer. It was into silence, therefore, that a further figure now walked. It was Burrow, the learned butler. Burrow was carrying a poker. He was conservatively attired in a striped nightshirt and a nightcap with a tassel. The effect, although grotesque rather than ghostly, had come pat upon Mrs. Mustard's assertion, and its effect was to evoke from Hallam Hillam—like Giles Tancock hitherto silent—a shrill burst of hysterical laughter. Hillam—Appleby observed— was also quivering all over. What was going on around him bore every appearance of being merely ludicrous, so he was entitled to mirth of a sort. But his nervous agitation spoke of something else as well. It had the feel of extreme bafflement. He was a little chap who in any circumstances would suggest something rather simian. At present he was like a monkey that just can't reach a peanut through the bars of its cage.

"I beg your pardon, sir," Burrow was saying placidly to his employer. He had evidently decided that the poker was not required. "Can I be of service in any way?"

116

"You can bring me a large glass of brandy." Terence produced this in a relaxed tone, as if something reasonable could at last be said. But then abruptly he was roaring again. "And some chloroform for this confounded woman."

"Spirits walk abroad at night," Mrs. Mustard reiterated, conscious of being brought back into the picture. "I am come to confront their questionable shapes. To establish rapport and reveal the truth. The obligation came to me in a dream."

Everybody gaped at Mrs. Mustard. Or everybody except Burrow, who was withdrawing from the library to fetch the brandy—and presumably the chloroform if it could be found. And at this point Inspector Denver made a heroic attempt to control the situation.

"Madam," he said to Mrs. Mustard, "I am concerned to reveal the truth too. Am I to understand that you have made your way to the library at this hour simply because it has . . . has been revealed to you in a dream that this possibly criminal affair can be elucidated by . . . by supernatural communications?"

"You are a sensible man," Mrs. Mustard said. "Precisely that. But it is not in vain. The profane vulgar are around us and have shattered the possibility of revelation. Adopt your own methods. Good night."

With this civil salutation Mrs. Mustard gathered her white samite around her, picked up her bag, and swept from the room. It wasn't before one of the constables had made to advance upon her, apparently with some dim notion of effecting an arrest. He was checked by his superior.

"Good night, madam," Denver said, and waited for the door to close behind the lady. "And now, gentlemen, my own methods may be resumed."

***

117

But the door immediately opened again. It was by that mysterious agency known only to upper servants, since Burrow, now framed in it, was bearing in both hands a large silver salver on which were disposed a decanter and a substantial array of rummers. A rapid count of these would have revealed him as considering that in the present exceptional circumstances even police constables might be reckoned entitled to their tot.

"The brandy, sir," Burrow said. "Would you wish me to remain?"

"Pour it out, man, and take some yourself." The sight of this recruitment had at once thrown Terence into a hospitable mood. "Mr. Denver here may want to have a word with you, blast him. Very naturally, no doubt." It was in some haste that Terence had added this last moderating remark. "Denver, go ahead and get through with it, like a good fellow. We've had it once already today, you know."

"Yesterday," Denver said.

"To be sure—yesterday." Terence had now managed a considerable gulp of brandy. "I'm damned if I knew what I was letting myself in for. It goes to show that you never can tell."

Perhaps only Appleby and Denver found this rather a strange remark. The two constables were occupied in making it conscientiously clear that they didn't drink on duty; Giles Tancock had withdrawn into a kind of wary reserve; Hillam was still in his obscure fever of bafflement or impatience; Burrow, although perhaps a man whom very little escaped, could not be detected as doing other than attend to the duties of his station.

"It should perhaps be made clear," Denver said, "that ¡standard police procedure has been in operation. Placing

118

under continued surveillance the site of a crime or suspected crime. Hence the presence of these officers and myself, concealed in the farthest alcove here in the library. Not ideal, since the position doesn't command the other alcoves. But better than nothing. And the measure is a perfectly normal one. I have no doubt Sir John will support me in that."

Appleby said nothing, but did venture on a slightly ambiguous nod. It was his private opinion that Denver had gone decidedly out on a limb. It was Terence Grinton who spoke.

"Dash it all, Denver," he said, "that's simply not good enough. I ought to have been—what's the blasted word?—apprised of your intention. You've been high-handed—very high-handed indeed."

"Well, sir, it has been this way." Denver seemed concerned to be conciliatory. "I've had to consider the possibility that Mr. Honeybath's discovery in this room, and the events immediately following upon that, in some fashion got in the way of something else. I have to admit it sounds rather an obscure idea, but somehow it stays with me. A matter of untransacted business, as it were."

"Untransacted fiddlesticks!" It was definitely as one of his roars that Grinton produced this: rather an alarmed and startled roar, Appleby felt. And Appleby felt, too, that Inspector Denver was showing considerable intellectual resource. It might even be that he had a grasp on the root of the matter.

"Well, sir, that's as may be." Denver was quite unperturbed. "But grant that I have this idea in my head, and you will see that if I had mentioned my intention to you, you would have been put at a disadvantage, in a manner of

119

speaking. You would have been the one person in this household in a position to avoid walking into what might be called an ambush. Because you knew it was there, you see."

This ingenious sophistry, although it would scarcely have stood up to cross-examination, served its purpose of confusing Terence Grinton, who mumbled something to the effect that Denver had better get on.

"Quite so, sir. And we must take the sequence of events. Here we are—three policemen hiding none too comfortably in an alcove and in total darkness. Then a light flicks on—a single light—and we see that Mr. Tancock has entered the library. Mr. Tancock, would that be right?"

"Of course it's right. I entered the library."

"Just so, Mr. Tancock. And why not? Mr. Grinton's son-in-law, perhaps experiencing a sleepless night, drops in to find a book to take him through the small hours. Nothing in it."

"Nothing at all," Tancock said. "As good a perhaps as any other chatter you could invent." Tancock had fixed on Denver the eye of a duellist. "Only it sounds bogus, and is meant to."

"But not the first book to come to hand," Denver continued. "Over there in a corner there's an unobtrusive little circular staircase leading down to a very large storage space beneath the library. No end of further books down there. And down Mr. Tancock goes."

"Perfectly true," Tancock said. "Down I go."

"And stay there for quite some time. We don't take any action, these two constables and myself. There's no way out from down there. You have to come up into the library again. So we can converse with Mr. Tancock later. But now

120

somebody else arrives. Mrs. Mustard. Now, we know about Mrs. Mustard. If there's anybody in this house I'm confident about it's Mrs. Mustard." Denver paused on this surprising remark, and then appealed to Appleby. "Wouldn't you say, sir?"

"Well, yes." Appleby was not very sure how to express himself. "Mrs. Mustard goes in for the mysterious, or at least the mystic, in a big way. But transparently, so to speak."

"Just so, sir. Harmlessly off her head. Like dancing or howling dervishes. They do turn up on the fringes of things from time to time. But not as really having a finger in the pie." Denver seemed unconscious of having plunged into a wealth of imagery. "She wanders around for quite some time, now within observation, and now poking into one alcove or another. For a moment it looks as if she is going to discover more than she bargains for, in the shape of those two constables and myself. But then in comes Mr. Hillam."

"In comes Mr. Hillam," Hillam said. It was at once clear that Hillam proposed taking a leaf out of Tancock's book and presenting an imperturbable front to the world. But perhaps he wasn't going to be so successful. He licked his lips. "Certainly I come in. So what?"

"More insomnia, perhaps," Denver said. "After all, it had been a disturbing day. But Mr. Hillam scarcely gets a chance to find a book. Discovering a light on seems to have disconcerted him a little, and perhaps he hasn't got his bearings in the library quite as Mr. Tancock has. He makes an indecisive move or two, and then becomes aware of Mrs. Mustard. Of course Mrs. Mustard wasn't pleased to encounter Mr. Hillam. He would disturb the aura, or the like. And Mr. Hillam, for some reason, wasn't at all pleased either. Within seconds, these two were ordering one another out of the room. It became a regular shindy. And in no time it was clear that Mrs. Mustard was winning."

"Nothing of the sort," Hillam said. "I deny it."

"There was Mr. Hillam," Denver went on implacably, "backing right into that great fireplace, and the lady waving her spiritualism or whatever right under his nose. And then he tripped up among all those mediaeval fire irons and fire dogs and the like with a most unholy clatter. That shook both of them a bit, and they began to sort themselves out. And arguing again. Then in came Mr. Grinton, roused by the din and brandishing a revolver. He says it was Mrs. Mustard made him really mad, but it seemed to me it was Mr. Hillam too. He fired the thing at the ceiling—I suppose with the idea of scaring the lights out of the two of them." Denver hesitated for a moment, perhaps conscious of having deviated into unofficial language. "Then up bobs Mr. Tancock from the basement, and out we come from our alcove. Sir John comes in. Mr. Burrow comes in with his poker. It's like an old play."

It seemed to Appleby an accurate comparison, although it would have been a little more specific if instead of "play" Denver had said "farce" or even "bedroom comedy": the sort of entertainment in which, through a sufficient variety of doors and even windows, people tumble inconveniently and surprisingly into one another's company. But reflection showed it to be a little simpler than that. The general effect had been crowded and bizarre, but the majority of the characters involved had turned up in the library with at least some colouring of a sober occasion. Denver and his constables had their duty to perform, although a night-long lurking in a house unbeknown to its owner was perhaps a shade over the odds. That Terence Grinton, having heard an unaccountable clangour in his library, should have hastened to investigate it, was entirely in order, except that then proceeding to fire off a revolver was indisputably to overreact to the situation. And that Mrs. Mustard, granted the pervasive weirdness of the universe she inhabited, should have thought to invocate spirits in a chamber from which a dead body had achieved a feat of bilocation was explicable after a fashion. Appleby himself was in roughly the same category as his host—as indeed was Burrow with his poker and his brandy. It was only Hillam and Tancock who had yet, as it were, to explain themselves.

Denver, being in no doubt about this, took up the point at once.

"Yesterday afternoon," he said, "something at present quite unaccountable took place in this room, and there was a further unaccountable event in the area one arrives in by going through that dummy door. There is a distinct possibility—to put it no higher than that—of some criminal activity being involved. So it is reasonable to investigate anything again unaccountable that takes place here in the library only a few hours later. And what I come to first, Mr. Tancock, is your entering it in the middle of the night."

"You've been good enough to explain that yourself, Inspector. I couldn't get to sleep, and I came to borrow a book." Tancock produced this with quite as much irony as was at all proper. "I called that bogus at once, and bogus it is."

"Then, sir, may we be favoured with the truth of the matter?"

"Certainly—although it may sound a little odd too. Also,

I must apologize in advance. It's true I couldn't get to sleep. I was worried about something, and it was a worry reflecting a certain lack of confidence in the police."

"Indeed, sir? Please continue."

"It was about this missing man—dead or sleeping. Sleeping, I told myself—and then disturbed by Mr. Honeybath, who fumbled at the fellow, and then cleared out."

Here Appleby interrupted.

"I think that significantly misrepresents Mr. Honeybath's behaviour. He satisfied himself, as he believed, that the man was dead, and then very properly sought help. But you'd better go on."

"Thank you. I will." Tancock paused, distinguishably with that effect of wariness which sometimes overtook him. "The man comes out of a heavy slumber. He may even have had a slight stroke—something of that kind. He staggers around in a bemused condition. I know it sounds very speculative, Inspector—but I'm simply telling you of a rather irrational state of worry I got into. Particularly when I remembered that treacherous little spiral staircase. Had the police been aware of it, and investigated the basement? I couldn't remember whether I'd heard anything about that. So I decided to come and take a look myself."

"So down you went," Denver said. "And remained down quite a long time. In fact, emerging only when there was the general shindy."

"You may express it that way. I felt a certain awkwardness in my situation."

"That seems not unlikely, sir. But as least you didn't find a corpse down there, or even a still living man in a grave condition."

"Happily, not."

And with this, Tancock gave an assured nod, and fell silent. He had explained himself, and that was it.

For a moment, at least, it was as if Denver showed himself baffled. It had been, in a fashion, a colourable yarn, and that it was all a shade phoney was a point that Tancock had cheerfully made himself. Very sensibly, Denver turned to his next man.

"Mr. Hillam," he asked. "can you tell me the reason for your own visit to the library? Were you suffering the same sort of anxiety as prompted Mr. Tancock to drop in?"

"Well, no—not exactly. Or rather, not at all." Unlike Tancock, Hillam displayed something like desperation. He hadn't, perhaps, a particularly inventive mind. "You see," he said, "I was very upset. It's not what one expects when one joins friends in the country for a quiet weekend. I got rather obsessed with the situation. Perhaps I *was* a little like Mr. Tancock in that." Hillam offered this hopefully, as if there might be something creditable in approximating his own condition to Tancock's after all. "Morbid curiosity," he said. "It does, I suppose, sound a bit wet. But I'm afraid that's the fact of the matter. I came in here out of morbid curiosity. And there was that dreadful woman. I rather lost my head, and we fell to shouting at each other. That was the whole story."

"The whole fairy tale, you mean!" Terence Grinton, who had amazingly kept silence for nearly ten minutes, now achieved one of his high-decibel performances. "Pilfering—that's what the fellow was up to." Grinton had turned to Denver. "Plain as a pikestaff. This room is full of rubbish that lunatic eggheads will pay money for. Not a doubt of it. Sermons and bawdy plays and travels in China. The little

125

brute invited himself down here—my wife told me as much—and is making away with whatever he can lay his hands on."

"It's an abominable lie! It's an insult!" Hillam was beside himself with rage—a condition in which, if he was an honest man, he had every right to be. "I don't give a damn for your rubbishing books. Not many of them would fetch sixpence on a barrow in the street, you ignorant baboon. And I shall, of course, leave your house this instant."

"And a bloody good riddance that will be. But it won't happen until these coppers have had a good hunt through your suitcases." Grinton was breathing heavily as a result of this exchange of amenities. "But no you won't either!" he suddenly shouted. "I'll give you in charge. Denver, I give this man in charge. Take him away and lock him up."

"Gentlemen, please compose yourselves." Denver spoke on a note of sharp authority. "Mr. Grinton, you cannot, as you express it, give Mr. Hillam in charge. Mr. Hillam, I understand your impulse to leave Grinton Hall at once. But I advise against it. It would be inconvenient."

What Hillam made of this was not apparent. For a moment, indeed, it was as if the contretemps had gone out of his head. He was glancing covertly round the library with what Appleby thought of as a lean and hungry look. So perhaps Grinton was right about him. But somehow Appleby doubted it. He sensed it as being, so to speak, not quite in the target area. But however that might be, this fantastic nocturne had gone on long enough.

"Grinton," Appleby said, "we must all be grateful for Mr. Denver's vigilance, and in my opinion he has this difficult situation well in hand. I suggest we all go back to bed, and start in again with clearer heads in the morning.

126

Everybody, I am sure, is anxious to see this uncomfortable mystery resolved."

These pacificatory noises (for they weren't much more than that) were offered with sufficient assurance to be of immediate effect. Burrow gathered up his rummers, and within five minutes the library was once more in darkness. Whether long-suffering constables were to continue lurking in it through the short remainder of the night was something nobody inquired about.

10

THE APPLEBYS, COMING DOWN TO BREAKFAST, MET
Charles Honeybath emerging from the drawing room.

"Nobody feeding yet," Honeybath said—and it was immediately apparent that, somewhat unaccountably, he was
in an almost buoyant mood. "They seem to keep latish
hours. By the way, was there some sort of disturbance in
the night? I thought I heard something."

"There was indeed," Appleby said. "I'll tell you about it
when we've had our coffee and feel a bit stronger."

"I thought I'd wait until somebody else appeared. One
always has a sense of being greedy if one presents oneself in
an empty room. So I thought I'd have another look round
in there." And Honeybath nodded towards the drawing
room. "It produced a real surprise. I must show you. Come
along."

Mildly astonished by this enthusiasm, Appleby and his
wife did as they were told. The curtains had been drawn
back in the drawing room, and there had already been a
tidy-round. Nevertheless, the place seemed to disapprove
of their presence at this inappropriate hour.

"All those watercolours," Honeybath said. "I have a
weakness for that kind of thing, and was wandering around

them yesterday evening. I came on a little watercolour by John Varley. Think of that! I wonder how a Grinton once possessed himself of it. Here it is! Isn't it tiptop?"

The Applebys admired the Varley.

"So in the night I found myself wondering whether there might be anything else out of the way: meaning not by deceased Grinton ladies. That's what brought me in ten minutes ago. And you'll never guess what I found." Honeybath was now in a state of great enjoyment. "So blessedly remote from that bothersome body! Come and look."

Obediently, the Applebys looked.

"Almost," Appleby said cautiously, "Chinese."

"Absolutely true!" Honeybath was delighted by this act of connoisseurship. "But of course it's by Claude. Just a wash drawing of what I take to be Tivoli. There's one very like it in the B.M. But the light, Judith, the light! Whenever I'm told that the Impressionists first really captured the stuff, I think of Claude. And here it happens in eight inches by six. However did those Grinton creatures come by *that?*"

"I think I can tell you," Judith Appleby said. "Or this book can." And she held up an octavo volume in aged but well-waxed leather. "John has just been reading it, and I'm returning it to its owner, Terence's Mr. Burrow. But you must have a look at the relevant place first, Charles. Here and now."

And thus Charles Honeybath became acquainted with *Reliquiae Grintonianae.*

From *Paris* it would appear that Mr. *Grinton* travelled direct to *Rome,* not by *Genoa* and the *Ligurian Sea,* but always in his own carriage as before, and with his own servants about him. It is a thing curious to remark that a man by nature so acquisitive as this *Ambrose Grinton* was yet regardless of the pitch of his quotidian expenses, and would live or journey, as the opportunity afforded him, in the style rather of a nobleman than a private gentleman. His route, which in all occupied many days, was by the *Colle del Moncenisio*, then still very horrid, since it pleased him to believe that he was thus following in the steps of *Hannibal*. The persuasion, although not puerile, was erroneous, since historiographers do now with one voice assert that the *Col du Clapier*, and not this of *Mont Cenis*, was the pass to tremble beneath the tread of the *Carthaginians* and their monstrous *Elephantes*. If disabused in this, he might have assuaged himself with the knowledge, little hidden from many schoolboys, one would suppose, that his path had assuredly been traversed by *Pepin the Short, Charlemagne,* and *Charles the Bald.* At least he had taken his own commodious carriage where no carriage road was, and this achievement may have contented him when, upon his arrival in the *Eternal City*, the vehicle had to be broken up incontinent.

Mr. *Grinton* had taken due care to provide himself with sundry letters introductory to good society in his new abiding place, and notably to M. *Béthune*, then French Ambassador to the Court of the Bp. of *Rome*. Although at home ever one decently attentive to his religious duties according to our Established Church, in Rome he *did as the Romans did*, entering with very little scruple into the highest *papistical* circles open to him. Thus by M. *Béthune* he was presented alike to Cardinals *Crescenzio* and *Bentivoglio*, and indeed to one *Maffeo Barberini*, who styled himself *Urban VIII* and claimed to occupy the throne of S. *Peter* himself.

It was a time at which such prelatical personages as these evinced much concern to exhibit themselves judicious *curiosi*, well-seen alike in the arts of antiquity and this *modern* age. Limners and statuaries, although no longer commanding the exalted regard and remuneration of a *Sanzio* or a *Buonarotti*, found ready patrons still among them. The

130

purse of Mr. *Grinton,* although seldom entirely empty, was inadequate to compete in this market with any amplitude. But he was ever on the alert to benefit as he could, and moreover it will be recalled that among his familiars he was jestingly referred to as *Autolycus Grinton,* after the snapper-up of unconsidered trifles created by the immortal *Shagsper.* This proclivity is well exhibited, and that to some effect of diversion, by his traffic with one *Gellée,* a *Frenchman* by extraction, and in *Rome* graduated painter from the less uncertain trade of pastry-cook.

The Cardinals and the Bp. alike stood patrons to *Gellée* (a name, Mr. *Grinton* gamesomely averred, well becoming one habituated to concocting kickshaws in a kitchen), known also as Le Lorrain, so that by the time of our *Autolycus'* visit he had become supereminent among such painters as devoted their genius to the limning of land-scapes in the Campagna of *Rome,* being in this more various, rich and rare than all others. Two characteristicks were remarked in him. He worked much in the very face of what he painted, sometimes in oils but more commonly with simpler materials, as if holding up to nature a mirror more faithful than the retirement of a *studio* could provide. He thus accumulated a wealth of *schizzi* (as the *Italians* say) to which he would turn when compositions of more magnitude were required of him, so that the floors of his dwelling were declared at times thick with these rapid starts not indeed of *fancy,* but of *observation.* Again, as his fame was augmented with the years, and that he might not be practised upon by counterfeiters of his own labours, he had the custom to take with pencil or with pen or the like drawings of his larger or elaborated works, thereby creating an ordered record of his authentic achievements. But in the pursuit of this design, eventually to be styled by him the *Libri di veritá,* he by no means always satisfied himself at a first or even a second endeavour. So from this characteristick there also arose a fine prodigality of *parerga* (as they may be styled) not very vigilantly guarded by their author. And it was the jest of many in *Rome* that England's Autolycus, who much frequented the *studio* of this jumpt-up kitchen-boy, seldom departed therefrom without having stuffed his pockets (which were capacious, following the fashion of that time) with sundry of these strays or waifs of art.

Winter approaching, Mr. *Grinton* next made his way to *Naples*. . .

"God bless my soul!" Still holding *Reliquiae Grintonianae* open in his hand, Honeybath jumped to his feet, crossed the drawing room, and stared again at the little Claude. Then he sat down on a sofa and composed himself. "John," he asked soberly, "just what does this mean?"

"It means that anybody acquainted with that book— including its owner, the admirable Burrow—could see there was a sporting chance that the chaos of the Grinton library harbours somewhere quite a number of drawings and the like by Claude Lorrain. If he came upon that one, framed and casually disposed among innumerable mediocre amateur watercolours in this room, he would feel confirmed in that view of the prospect. Of course I've heard of Claude's *Liber Veritatis*. How many drawings does it run to?"

"A hundred and ninety-five, I think, plus another five that are not related to known paintings. The whole lot were tucked away at Chatsworth for I don't know how long. But now, of course, they're in the British Museum. Incidentally, I don't think Claude can have got going very seriously on the *Liber Veritatis* idea until after this rascally Ambrose Grinton's time. And it isn't likely that the Reverend Simon Upcott was much of an art historian. But in general his yarn sounds likely enough."

132

"Supposing," Judith asked, "there really are say a dozen *schizzi* or whatever by Claude hidden away there in the library, what, approximately, might they be worth?"

"The moon. No other possible answer." Honeybath spoke firmly. "That fellow Tancock would tell you the market for such things has gone completely mad. Claude is important, and will always be important. And he's dead. So the theory of scarcity value operates. Buy him, lock him up in a vault, and the theory guarantees you won't lose your money."

"I'm not quite certain about the guarantee," Appleby said. He was somewhat sceptical of his friend's command of political economy. "But it's certain that the value of such a group of drawings would make the value of anything else hidden away in that library look simply silly. Short, say, of the manuscript of *Hamlet Prince of Denmark*."

"Surely," Honeybath asked, "it has been irresponsible of this man Burrow to have been possessed of this information and not to have informed his employer?"

"Oh, I don't think so," Judith said. Judith seemed to have a sense of Terence Grinton's butler as under her own protection. "Burrow is very much an autodidact, and when he read about that stuff lying around a studio floor the penny mightn't drop with him. I suggest we go to breakfast."

They moved towards the door, but Honeybath came to a halt beside the little display cabinet containing the Indian divinities.

"Dear me!" he said. "I've just remembered something."

"You have a talent for it, Charles." Appleby halted too. "What is it, this time? Not more about that dead man's clothes?"

"No, no. An incident in this room, yesterday evening.

133

What has put me in mind of it is those little bronzes. It may be nothing very significant. Disturbing all the same."

"Out with it."

"Well, it was when I noticed the little watercolour by Varley. It was a surprising discovery, lost in the middle of all this family art. I was with Tancock and Hillam, you know. And I was quite excited. I said to them something like, 'Let's see if there's anything more of the same sort,' and walked on down the room. But Hillam called out to me to have a look at those Indian things, and I saw at once that they are interesting. Hillam started giving names to them, and then that bell went to tell us to wash and brush up for dinner."

"And your previous movement had been such," Appleby asked, "that continuing it would have brought you face to face with Claude's Tivoli?"

"Yes, indeed."

"So you think that perhaps Hillam didn't want you to see it?"

"Well, I do now. But there wasn't the slightest impression of anything of the sort at the time. I mean anything like the man being flustered or alerted, or speaking abruptly. So my suspecting anything is a matter of hindsight."

"The question seems to be," Judith said, "what might have succeeded upon your noticing such an unexpected thing in this room. Suppose that Hillam is acquainted with *Reliquiae Grintonianae,* and got himself invited here to Grinton as a consequence. He can't know who else is, or is not, similarly acquainted with it. Its very suggestive information may just conceivably be latent, as it were, in somebody's mind; and if on the strength of your indeed spotting the drawing you start talking about Claude and asking questions here and there, the subject may gain a promi-

134

nence inimical to the success of Hillam's dark design. If he has a dark design. John, do you think he has a dark design?"

"Yes," Appleby said. "I do. Or, if he hasn't, he has had. A complex situation may have got out of hand from his point of view, and he is thinking twice about remaining in the fray. That's just one possibility. There are others. And now for breakfast."

11

A COMPLEX SITUATION, APPLEBY REPEATED TO HIMSELF over his bacon and egg. Commonplace in its elements, possibly, but unusual in what might be called its concatenations, and distractingly bizarre in some of its trimmings. Quite a handful for Inspector Denver.

The Grinton library as subject to two independent if confusingly interwoven schemes of depredation. A long-term one and a short-term one.

Giles Tancock, the auctioneer who knows the right price for a rare book. Who, although Terence Grinton's son-in-law, has no great expectations in that quarter. Who is hard up, likely enough, since his wife has expensive and rather silly plans for their children. Tancock no doubt visits his parents-in-law frequently; he knows all about the library and its history; he knows how completely neglected and unfrequented it is. So he falls into the way of quietly tracking down and abstracting such fairly valuable books as are likely to be scattered around amid its chaos. Quite soon he is being thoroughly systematic about this. He brings in the catalogues of antiquarian booksellers as a kind of *aide-mémoire,* and tackles the enormous quantity of stuff down in the cellarage.

The one day (yesterday in fact) something distinctly awkward happens in the library—although whether he is directly implicated in it or not is at present an unsolved question. And suddenly in the night he realizes that he must have left one of those catalogues behind him. A very recent catalogue, as its number will at once betray. Probably carrying his fingerprints. Awkward. He gets out of bed and steals down to retrieve it. While he is down below, first Mrs. Mustard arrives, and then Hillam. Fracas! Enter Terence, who promptly fires his pistol. Tancock decides to emerge, and when he does so makes the discomfiting discovery that police have been lurking around all the time. Finally he spins them a yarn that has at least a certain ingenuity to recommend it.

But the yarn involves the missing body. And the missing body is the crux. And this conjectural history of Giles Tancock affords no explanation of it. No place for the body. Checkmate.

Appleby got up and poured himself another cup of coffee.

Second scheme of depredation: the short-term one, and susceptible of being outlined very succinctly. Hallam Hillam, some sort of art historian. Probably from *Reliquiae Grintonianae,* but perhaps through other professional researches, he learns about Ambrose—or Autolycus—Grinton and his thieved Claudes. Cadges an invitation to Grinton. Spots the Claude in the drawing room and knows he isn't on a fool's errand. Like Tancock, is under some sufficiently powerful impulse to risk a nocturnal visit to the library despite the afternoon's startling episode there and the subsequent visit of police. It doesn't seem possible that he has any precise information about where the drawings may be found. There is, of course, nothing about that in the

137

Reverend Simon Upcott's book. Nevertheless, Hillam contrives to feel himself on the very brink of success. He renders an irritated and thwarted impression, all the same. A jumpy chap. But if this is the whole of his story, the dead man is again left out in the cold. So once more checkmate is the last word.

Appleby had arrived at this bleak conclusion when he became aware of Burrow's voice murmuring discreetly in his ear.

"The telephone, Sir John. Mr. Denver the policeman."

"Appleby here."

"Denver speaking. We've found the body, Sir John."

"Dear me!" Appleby was constrained to this almost Honeybath-like response by a feeling of something ominous in the air. This chap Denver was reporting to him precisely as if he, Appleby, were in charge of the case. It was absurd and most irregular. Nevertheless, Appleby succumbed at once to what his wife was so fond of borrowing from *Love's Labour's Lost* to describe. A *trick of the old rage* . . . "An American's body, I take it?"

"Sir!"

"Keen observation, Inspector. But Mr. Honeybath's, not mine. Where has it turned up?"

"At the parish church, Sir John. Or, rather, in its graveyard."

"Do you mean somebody has been burying it in the night?"

"Not exactly that. I'm wondering whether you would care to"—Denver hesitated for a moment, and then plunged at a bold word—"investigate?"

"Yes." (Honesty, after all, is the best policy.)

138

"I'll send a car at once. If, perhaps, you'd care just to take a stroll down the drive."

"Why the dickens should I do that?"

"Well, sir, I think we oughtn't to advertise too much— not just at the moment we shouldn't—to the Grintons and their other guests."

"Sound policy, Denver. I'll set out in five minutes."

So Appleby had to acknowledge to himself, once more, that Denver was a thoroughly good officer. With an uncommon puzzle on his hands, he was only acting sensibly in tapping a considerable fund of experience in such matters when it came his way. Appleby returned to the breakfast room, murmured to Judith, got into his overcoat, and set off in search of his unnecessary conveyance. The church could be no distance away—and indeed he recalled Honeybath as telling him there was a short cut to it from the back of the house. But no doubt it was a matter of punctilio with Denver that he should arrive in style at this new seat of the inquiry. There was a young uniformed constable in the driver's seat, and on Appleby's approach he leapt from it with parade-ground smartness. He had clearly been told that he was going to act as chauffeur to a very great man indeed.

"Well now," Appleby said cheerfully as he got into the front seat, "have you been involved in this discovery of a dead man?"

"Yes, sir. I found him, as a matter of fact. A bit of a shock, really."

"It comes to us all, sooner or later. Sooner, with me. I hadn't been on the beat a week when there suddenly was my first corpse. Outside a pub. A pool of blood. Now tell me about this one."

"As I drive, sir?"

"Certainly not. Now, and giving your whole mind to it."

"Very good, sir." The young man had taken this well. "I live in the village—marrying into it, you may say."

"You got married to a girl from here, so they found you a house at once and told you to be the village bobby."

"About that sir, although the term now seems to be neighbourhood policeman."

"Encouraged to be friendly all round."

"Just that, sir. With some of them it can be a bit of a strain. But I like talking to the kids. And it's why, once a week or thereabout, I go into the Grinton Arms for a pint and a chat."

"Without your funny hat."

"Oh yes, sir, of course. Off-duty kit. And yesterday evening I got talking to an old chap called Bill Mace—or he got talking to me. He has a cottage near the church, and since ever anybody can remember he's been saying he has lived in it for eighty-seven years. It's the only dwelling that has a view of the churchyard. He's an unreliable old gossip is Bill Mace—particularly once a month, which is as often as he can afford to get drunk. But when he starts talking to me I always try to listen. You never know."

"A great truth in our walk of life, constable. Yes?"

"Earlier in the evening, he said, he'd seen a funny thing: a gent going into the church. He said a gent, but may have meant actually a gentleman."

"I see." Appleby received this mysterious remark seriously as an attempt at precision. "There doesn't seem anything particularly funny in a man going into a church."

"It's more commonly women nowadays."

"I suppose that's true. Devotion has become women's work. But what arrested the attention of this Bill Mace?"

140

"He was carrying a kettle and a frying pan."

"Mace was?"

"No, sir. The gent. Presently he came out again, but returned within a couple of minutes carrying a bed. He took that into the church too. A folding bed, it was."

"And then?"

"Mace says he drew down his blind. He says he was afraid he was seeing things. It's a trouble with him now and then."

"So he took no further action?"

"No, sir. But I did."

"Good. Go on."

"I downed the remainder of my pint—it wouldn't have looked right if I hadn't—and went straight over to the church. There was nothing out of the way in it—so it looked as if Mace had been seeing things, just as he said. But I tried the vestry, which leads off one side of the chancel. The vicar never locks it up, although I've warned him more than once. Well, there the bed was—and the kettle and frying pan and a fold-up table and a chair I knew didn't belong there as well. It wasn't very accountable."

"Clearly not." Appleby paused. "And what, constable, did you do then?"

"I've been taught that when you come on one unaccountable thing you should lose no time before looking for others. So I cast around. That's how I came to look into the charnel house."

"Into the *what?*"

"It's what the vicar calls it, although it's no more than the shed where the man who looks after the churchyard and digs the graves keeps his tools and things. Except that when he turns up bones—and once or twice a skull, I believe—he stores them there. Thinking of them as

141

curiosities, I suppose. They ought to be buried again at once. And perhaps with the vicar saying a prayer over them. I wouldn't know. But there the body was."

"And what did you do?"

"I went straight home and got Mr. Denver on the telephone, sir. And that's all. Of my part in the thing, I mean."

"I think Mr. Denver will agree with me that you didn't do badly. And now we can move off."

The body had been moved out of the charnel house (which did in fact shelter a little pile of bones) and into a police van of sombre character in which it was to be whisked away for what Inspector Denver called forensication. Appleby contented himself with a look at the dead man's features and found them uninformative: during the night hours it was to be presumed that their internal chemistry had wiped out the expression that had so vividly struck Charles Honeybath.

"No external signs of violence immediately apparent," Denver said. "Of course we'll know more in a few hours' time. As for the clothes, they're American beyond question. There's the label of a New York store, or tailor, on the inside of the jacket. That's the only scrap of documentation, though. All the pockets turned out and emptied. But this is an odd sort of hiding place, wouldn't you say? Gruesome."

"Or at least fantastic. Have you discovered how often this shed is likely to be entered?"

"At this time of year, with nothing much going on in the way of tidying up the churchyard, not all that often. Probably not until the fellow concerned has a burial on his hands."

"What about the church, where your young man tells me

those scraps of furniture were found by him tucked away in the vestry?"

"Every second Sunday only. The vicar has three other rural parishes on his hands, and manages only one early-morning communion and one matins in the month. No demand, he'd tell you—and he never bobs in just on his own. Strange, that—don't you think?"

"What I chiefly think, Denver, is that this has the character of a holding operation: a temporary cache while taking a second breath in an alarming situation. But another thing: why both shed and vestry? There would have been plenty of room, surely, for both the corpse and the paraphernalia in either. Perhaps it's a pointer to something in the character of the operator."

"How so, sir?"

"My guess is that he made two journeys. One with the body and one with the furniture. And the body first, on a trip Mr. Bill Mace didn't spot. When he came back with the furniture—the existence of which he may have been unaware of at the time of bringing the body—he suddenly felt he didn't want to face the body again. So he thought of the vestry, and dumped the stuff there."

"And he knew the lie of the land, Sir John, and about the infrequency of the services here. A local man—like, for instance, Mr. Grinton himself."

"Aren't you being rather determined, Denver, not to lose sight of Mr. Grinton?"

"Certainly I am, Sir John. I've no mind to lose sight of anybody." Denver said this stiffly, but at once added, "You've produced a picture, sir. Not a doubt about that. I'm most grateful to you."

"The chap who will be grateful to the police for finding

the corpse is Mr. Honeybath. He can't any longer be suspected of having dealings with little green men."

"I never thought Honeybath was off his head." Denver was a shade indignant again. "But I did think that his supposed dead man might be ambulant—capable of packing up and making off under his own steam. Do you happen to have heard, Sir John, of anything of particularly high value that may be tucked away in the library up there?"

This sudden and penetrating question took Appleby by surprise.

"Yes," he said at once. "A group of small paintings or drawings by a French artist of the seventeenth century, Claude Lorrain."

"Good Lord!" Denver had taken the measure of this at once. "That's just something more that it's hard to believe. Who knows about them?"

"Certainly not Mr. Grinton. Just possibly, his butler. Assuredly my wife and myself. And, among the present guests up there, almost certainly Mr. Hillam."

"Well, I'm definitely not losing sight of *him*. That was a poor show he put up in the library last night, wouldn't you say? Not that the same wasn't true of the other fellow as well. The son-in-law. Tancock. Mightn't he know about the Claudes too?"

"He might. Or he might know about something else. Or they may be hand in glove with one another, although they gave no hint of it. But neither of them seems to me to guide us to the dead man. Where did this American come from, and why did he come?"

"For the matter of that, Sir John, why did he go—and why had he been camping, if it had been he, in that little room behind the library? No end of questions. What seems fairly clear to me is that it all ended up with an effort to remove the slightest trace of a crime. And it looks as if it were an effort made by somebody unaware of Mr. Honeybath having come upon the body, or of you and Mr. Honeybath having come upon the camping kit. But for these two things, there would be no mystery at this moment. There would only be a body and some junk in hideaways of tolerable security, waiting to be permanently disposed of at the first safe opportunity."

"Yes, Inspector—only I'm not quite sure about the crime—or at least about its having been at all a bumper one. We've found the corpse, but is it very substantially what the lawyers call a *corpus delicti*, evidence of a major breach of the law? There may be light on that when you get your police surgeon's report."

"In a preliminary and informal way, Sir John, that may be within an hour or two. And I'll let you know as soon as it comes in. But the dead man's identity may be a real headache. Missing persons have a way of not being missed. Particularly, as you know, if they happen to be foreigners. Shall I get that constable to drive you back to the house?"

"Thank you, no. I think I'll walk. And perhaps take a turn round the place. I'll contact you if anything comes into my head. Or anything that at all looks like standing up."

So Appleby went strolling through what Terence Grinton called his park. It wasn't really much of a park, since the ancient manorial status of Grinton was still evident in the fact that what fairly closely surrounded the house was the territory of the original home farm, around which now extended the fields of further farms which the Grintons had progressively acquired for themselves over several centuries. Appleby thus strolled for quite some time, having thinking to do.

The identity of the intrusive American, now dead, would no doubt emerge in time. It was less important than his role. With just what—and perhaps with whom—did he tie up? It seemed unlikely that he could be in any way connected with the shifty Hallam Hillam. About Hillam there was no doubt. He had somehow got wind of the possible treasure trove of Claudes, and he had wished himself upon the Grintons, or at least upon Dolly Grinton, as a result. He was entirely a newcomer on the scene. And he believed himself—Appleby was almost certain of this—to be on the brink of successful depredation when baffled and incommoded by unexpected complications in the situation. It was, of course, possible that he had in some way acted rashly as a result, and was implicated in the main mischief under review. So it wouldn't be quite prudent to write him off as, so to speak, a peripheral phenomenon. But the likelihood lay that way.

Giles Tancock was a different fish. Depredation was his line too, but it was on a long-term basis. With those catalogues in his pocket, he was in the habit of prowling his father-in-law's library, and unobtrusively milking it. Perhaps his wife Magda knew or suspected this; to Honeybath she had acknowledged herself to be nervous, even apprehensive, of the now police-infested Grinton scene. It was a minor point. What was significant was her husband's movements—and even, perhaps, something in his character. Had he been in any sort of collusion with the dead man—either for some time, or abruptly drawn into something of the sort by an unforeseen turn of events? He was a more resourceful person than Hillam: his performance during that nocturnal episode in the library, when in a tight

146

place, had been evidence of a certain power of quick thinking.

What else was to be said about Tancock? Looked at hard, the notion of his being in any sort of settled partnership with the American just didn't wash. Tancock's behaviour was commonplace in a shabby fashion; the American's was almost too fantastic to be believed. What could bring a man to consume hasty Welsh Rabbits in a lurking place in another man's house? Find an answer to that conundrum, Appleby told himself, and this weekend mystery was solved.

As he became aware of this conclusion he became aware, too, that he was about to be joined by another guest taking the morning air, Magda Tancock's former tutor, the learned Miss Arne. She greeted him briskly, and fell into step with him at once—not, it presently appeared, without designs upon him.

"Chilly but no puddles," she said. "So we can walk right round the gardens, Sir John, and call it the day's constitutional."

"An odd use of the word," Appleby returned. "Would it perhaps have been university slang?"

"Definitely—and a sort of academic ancestor of jogging. A constitutional of forty minutes every day was *de rigueur* at Oxford in the 1880s. What is this I hear of further absurdities in the library during the night?"

"They occurred." Appleby felt that this was a little bleak and off-putting. "Our friend Mrs. Mustard was involved. She appears to have believed that the mysterious affair of the afternoon might be cleared up by means of supernatural solicitation. Nothing came of the idea."

"I am sorry to hear it. An unresolved fatality is an unsatisfactory thing to leave behind one after a quiet weekend

147

in the country. I suspect you, Sir John, of having your own views about it all."

"Well, yes. But they are inchoate, so far." Miss Arne, Appleby reflected, drew ink-horn terms from one willy-nilly. But he also felt that conceivably the lady's special knowledge might be tapped with advantage. "I've certainly been wondering about that library—meaning the contents, not the building. It must be representative of a good many country-house libraries—except as being even less explored than most. What are the chances of such a place containing first-class bibliographical treasures mouldering unsuspected on the shelves?"

"Substantial. It is rather, you know, as with paintings and the like. Prices have been going through the roof."

"Have they, indeed?" Appleby was startled by this whiff, as it were, from the Claude Lorrain world.

"I heard of a curious instance quite recently. It was recounted to me by an old friend, the Savilian Professor of Astronomy. He was visiting a former schoolfellow—actually an impoverished landowner rather like our present host. They rummaged together in just such a library as Mr. Grinton's—not without hopes of the kind one might nourish here, since at one time there had been learning in the family. What they came upon was called, I think, *Uranographia Britannica, or Exact View of the Heavens,* by one Bevis, a Fellow of the Royal Society. It dated from the mid-eighteenth century, and was in good condition. It gained for its unsuspecting owner five thousand pounds. Half a dozen such random treasures, as you call them, would bring in a very useful sum of money indeed."

"Decidedly so." Appleby felt that he must revise his ideas. That book by the Reverend Mr. Shaw on the antiquities of Staffordshire was small beer compared with this.

Think of that American. A trip across the Atlantic and much clandestine activity would be amply rewarded by the discovery of a few companions to one Bevis. You could pick up Richard Jefferies' *Bevis*, an immortal work, for a few shilling from a barrow, but *Uranographia* Bevis was a different matter. A mad world, my masters.

12

WHILE APPLEBY CONVERSED WITH THE INFORMATIVE lady, Honeybath had been conversing with Burrow. This was because Lady Appleby, by way of passing the ball around, had suggested that it was he who should return *Reliquiae Grintonianae* to its owner. Burrow was rinsing decanters. But behind him, on row upon row of shelves, stood what bore much the appearance of the working library of a scholar. As Honeybath sought permission to enter, Burrow glanced at an elegant bracket clock on his mantelshelf. But this was certainly not by way of an uncivil hint that he was busy; rather it was to assure himself that the morning hour was not yet sufficiently advanced to admit of his offering his visitor a glass of Madeira.

"I hope I don't disturb you, Mr. Burrow," Honeybath said. "Lady Appleby let me have this book, and suggested that I bring it back to you. It is extremely interesting."

"To the family and family friends, certainly, sir." Burrow was again being entirely civil; he was acknowledging Honeybath's position within a privileged circle. "Lady Appleby, as you know, is a Raven. Very good people, sir, and variously distinguished in a number of fields from time to time. A little like the Grintons in that. You will recall, for example, her ladyship's cousin, Mr. Everard Raven, editor both of *The New Millennium Encyclopaedia* and of *The Revised and Enlarged Resurrection Dictionary.* Each is a work of very substantial learning. And the Ravens, of course, are related to the Mounteagles. It is thus that her ladyship may trace her descent from Charles Martel."

"Is that so?" Honeybath tried to remember something impressive to say about Charles Martel, but could recall only that he was a terrible swell who hammered the Moors at the battle of Tours in 732. Commanding this date was rather impressive after a fashion, but he doubted whether the jingle would appeal to this studious butler. So he tried something else. "Is Mr. Grinton's library," he asked, "particularly rich in that fascinating field of genealogy?"

"Well, sir, the library is much in all our minds at the moment."

"Yes, indeed." Thus firmly indicted as having asked a fishing question, Honeybath opted for frankness. "Although not intimate with the family, Mr. Burrow, and merely being privileged to stay here as the result of a professional engagement, I am a good deal worried myself."

"The unexpected discovery of a dead man, even if a total stranger, must certainly be distressing." Burrow might almost have been the family doctor. "Nothing could be more natural. The reaction itself is not to be worried about unduly. But the surrounding circumstances"—and Burrow frowned momentarily, as if aware of having perpetrated a tautology—"are disturbing, without a doubt. As to genealogy, so far as it concerns the Grintons, one would expect to find any relevant materials largely in manuscript form. But Mr. Grinton is peculiar about anything of the sort. And so, I believe, was his father before him. My own father, as you may have heard, sir, was in the late Mr. Grinton's service."

And like son, like father, if one may so vary the old expression. Neither of them reading men, Mr. Honeybath. And particularly impatient of written records. I believe my present employer might well tell you that nothing done by hand is likely to be of the slightest value."

"Yes," Honeybath said. "He well might."

"Naturally, sir, being of what may be termed a historical turn of mind myself, I deprecate such an attitude. It would be a great satisfaction to me, you see, to achieve an unpretending monograph on the history of the family."

"An excellent project, Mr. Burrow." It was with unflawed respect that Honeybath now regarded this unusual menial. "But you find difficulties in your way?"

"Very much so, I am sorry to have to report. Mr. Grinton does not care for any kind of investigation in the library. Every few years he has in a professional firm to do a clear up. If any scribbled rubbish—as Mr. Grinton expresses it—gets in the way of their vacuum cleaners, they have instructions to chuck it in the wastepaper baskets."

"Dear me! I would not willingly criticize a host, Mr. Burrow, but it does seem a regrettable attitude."

"Indeed, yes, Mr. Honeybath. And I ought to say at once that Mr. Grinton has on several occasions been very indulgent to my own interests. But less so, perhaps, of recent months. Formerly, I did move about the library from time to time, and even ventured to make a number of transcripts of documents that appeared to be of particular interest in relation to that brief history of the family—a mere dream though I fear it to be."

"I hope, Mr. Burrow, that it won't turn out to be only that. Of course you have had a predecessor in the clergyman who compiled the *Reliquiae Grintonianae*. He records a good deal of family eccentricity, if the term isn't disparag-

152

ing, but he doesn't come down much beyond Ambrose Grinton, who is certainly worth commemorating. What about Jonathan, for instance, the friend of Alexander Pope: have you come on any records of him?"

"Ah, Mr. Jonathan!" For the first time during this peculiar interview, Burrow hesitated to proceed. He even bore the appearance of a sorely tempted man. "I don't know that Mr. Jonathan can be said to have been—or at least to have remained—exactly a friend of Pope's. And to fall out with Pope was injudicious, to say the least."

"So I understand, Mr. Burrow." Honeybath ventured to lapse into silence after making this brief comment, and rely upon a glance of bold expectation that more excitement was to come. And come it did.

"Mr. Jonathan Grinton kept a journal from time to time, all of which I am afraid has since gone into one of those wastepaper baskets. But of certain passages I ventured to make transcripts a good many years ago—but sparingly, since I knew that Mr. Terence Grinton would consider it a very idle employment. Some of these passages chronicle Alexander Pope's sojourn at Grinton. Or perhaps I should rather say his departure. The visit cannot be said to have gone well."

"Is that so? I believe it to be notorious that Pope was a difficult man."

"And a dangerous one, Mr. Honeybath. It is within my recollection that one of the critics has described him as a metrical death adder."

"A phrase perhaps a little on the picturesque side—don't you think, Mr. Burrow? But I remember enough of Pope's invective powers to understand what is meant. Did he fall to satirizing this Jonathan Grinton?"

"It would appear that he did. But Mr. Jonathan may be

said to have fallen to satirizing him in turn. He recorded in his journal—and this is among the excerpts I ventured to make—a somewhat ludicrous character of his departed guest." For the second time Burrow distinguishably hesitated. But the scholar's vanity took control. "I wonder, Mr. Honeybath, whether you would care to cast an eye over it? I believe my transcript to be of very tolerable accuracy. Such operations, like the decanting of wine, require to be undertaken with the greatest care."

"I'd like to see it very much," Honeybath said. But he was in fact a little doubtful about what was being suggested. Nothing if not a punctilious man, he reflected that it was in a sense Terence Grinton's property that was concerned: Burrow's transcript but—as it might be expressed—Terence's copyright. It wasn't quite proper—decidedly it wasn't quite proper—to come by this backstairs view of the ancestral Jonathan. But to his credit as a person of good sense, Honeybath brushed these misgivings aside. "If it isn't inconvenient," he said.

But Burrow already had a key in his hand. It proved to be the key not of some unremarkable drawer but of the capacious old-fashioned iron safe in which he no doubt locked up nightly the greater part of the Grinton family silver. The safe itself contained drawers, and from one of these Burrow drew a leatherbound notebook of substantial bulk. He opened it with care, turned with due deliberation to the appropriate entry, and gravely handed it to his visitor.

It was thus that Charles Honeybath acquainted himself with an excerpt from the private papers of Jonathan Grinton.

Sept. 11. 1718.
Departed from *Grinton* this Day my good friend *Matt.*

154

Prior, lepidissimus poeta, for his late-purchased Seat of *Down Hall* in Essex, come to him (as he confided to me) in part through the Munificence of my lord of Oxford. No Daughter of Mnemosyne is other than a costly Mistress, and no Man more wretched than the Poet of the Proverb with his *empty purse.* Alas! when I see an ingenious Man set up for a *meer poet,* and steer his Course through Life without the Rudder of at least a few *paternal acres* to his name, I give him up as one *prick'd down by Fate, for misery and misfortune.* 'Tis something unaccountable, but one wou'd incline to think there's some indispensible Law, whereby Poverty and Disappointment are entail'd upon Poets. Our own *Cowley,* if I mistake not the Story, despite a small Competency provided for him by the Earl of St. Albans and Duke of Buckingham, cou'd not purchase himself so much as a little House with a small Garden to it, when he made his *retreat from the world.* I wou'd not alledge all this to disswade any noble *Genius* to pursue this *Art* as a little pretty Divertisment, but where 'tis made the very *trade of life,* I am pretty positive the Man's in the wrong Box.

And heer I am put in Mind of *Alex. Pope* the Linen Draper's Son, a poor misshapen Creature by me entertained at *Grinton* not many Years' past, and a most precocious Master (be it admitted) of the new *heroical verse* perfected by *Sir Jn Denham* and *Edmund Waller* of Beaconsfield Bucks Esquire. How unlike his Departure from this House to that of honest *Matt.* today! Discovering in the young Man's Pate a most *megalomaniacal maggot,* to wit the Translating the entire Works of *Homer* by the said *Pope* through Subscription of all the Nobility and Gentry of this Kingdom, I judged it my Duty, since myself a Person of Consideration and in His Majesty's Commission, to endeavour admonishing the Lad and teaching him *the twitch of his tether.* And he not caring for this Correction, and evidencing the same with no proper Sense of his *due station* but rather with Expressions of no little Insolence, I was constrained to say to him, *Ne sutor*

155

ultra crepidam, which Utterance the Wretch taking to
reflect upon the mechanick Employment of his Progenitor,
presently flew into a Rage, withdrew into his own Chamber,
and there sulk'd for two Days and Nights entire. From
thence he emerged to hand me a Paper, or rather several
Quires of such, full of *abominable libel and scurrility* concerning myself and all belonging to me. With the Restraint
proper to a Gentleman I read the first hundred Verses of
this *odious composure* before crumpling up the same and
casting it from me in a Passion. Whereupon, regarding me
with *insolent malice,* he declared that *if ever he were
minded to celebrate his residence at* Grinton *in publick
prints it would be in some such form as that that he had
given me a sight of.*

I did no more, upon this *vast impertinence,* than summon
my Steward and bid a Conveyance be prepar'd, saying that
Mr. *Pope* was minded to leave *Grinton* forthwith. No
further Word past between us. The upstart Fellow's ingrate
Scribblings I was prompted to consign to the Flames forthwith. But I reflected that, were he similarly to misconduct
himself in other Houses, and thus become in very Truth a
publick pest, they might serve as Evidence of *habitual
knavery* if presented in a Court of Law. So I lock'd them up,
and heer in this new-built Library where I compose these
brief Memorials from Time to Time they somewhere reside.
I have (need I say) small List to a further Perusal of them.

It was by no means in utter bewilderment that Charles
Honeybath handed this curious document back to its
transcriber. It was rather with a sense (if the phrase be
possible) of cloudy illumination. Light had broken, in
fact—although he didn't quite see on what. Dimly he felt
the presence in this mysterious affair of some highly
academic person. Burrow himself was almost that—
although distinctly of amateur status. Honeybath recalled

Appleby talking (with an ill-judged facetiousness, as he had felt it at the time) of a pernoctating and professorlike individual as lurking in the hinterland of the affair of the disappearing corpse. *A substantial and hitherto unknown early satire by Alexander Pope:* that surely among the learned would be quite something. Unearthed in holograph, it would also, without doubt, be of high pecuniary value. A man might even commit murder in order to possess himself of it.

With this final alarming thought in his mind, Honeybath glanced cautiously at Burrow. Burrow was replacing his document in its drawer, and closing and locking the safe again. Just what thoughts were in the fellow's head? Had he ever himself hunted for the missing poem, so confidently asserted by Jonathan (although nearly three centuries ago) to "reside" in this library still? *Had he even found it?*

On second thoughts, this last speculation was of course wholly implausible. Were the thing in Burrow's possession now, or had he long ago possessed himself of it and quietly parted with it to considerable advantage, he would certainly not have produced that transcript for a stray guest's entertainment or edification. But this didn't mean that he was not possessed of more information, or substantially grounded conjecture, than he had admitted to. Perhaps he could be judiciously sounded out. And a little further conversation, after all, seemed proper and even essential as a sequel to what Honeybath had just been shown.

"That is certainly a most interesting and amusing document, Mr. Burrow. But surely I am not the only person you have shown it to? What about Mr. Grinton himself?"

"I have never brought it to his attention, sir. It is Mr. Grinton's foible to hold in very poor esteem such of his

157

ancestors as interested themselves in anything other than field sports. It may be said of him that he is cast in an antique mould; that one might find him, in a manner of speaking, in the pages of the novelist Henry Fielding."

"I suppose that's so." Honeybath found himself disconcerted by this further disclosure of the reach of Burrow's literary interests. "But he must know about Jonathan, and about Pope having been here, and similar episodes of the same kind, at least in a general way."

"Very true, sir. I believe Mr. Grinton has indeed heard of Pope. But he will not, I judge, have been tempted to look into him."

"I can well believe it. But about that document—that transcription of yours. You must have shown it at one time or another to somebody else as well as myself?"

"To the best of my recollection, Mr. Honeybath, only to Professor Hagberg."

Honeybath, although prompted to demand, "And who the devil is Professor Hagberg?" contented himself by repeating "Hagberg?" on a note of mild inquiry. But Burrow was clearly disappointed in him.

"The eminent American scholar, sir. He called—I suspect without introduction—on Mr. Grinton some months ago, and was clearly one of those university people who express an interest from time to time in the sporadic literary or artistic connections of certain of the Grintons. Mr. Grinton dislikes them on sight, I need hardly say." For the first time in this remarkable conversation, Burrow allowed himself a certain dryness of manner as he said this. "The meeting went badly. I regret to say it, but Mr. Grinton was downright rude to the man. I endeavoured to do what I could."

"And just what was that?"

"I ventured to enter a little into conversation with him while helping him into his overcoat. Most affable and conversable, the Professor was. The name of Pope came up."

"Did it, indeed?"

"Since I was already aware, sir, of Professor Hagberg's main field of research."

"So one thing led to another?"

"Just so, sir. The Professor was kind enough to join me in this pantry, and before he left I showed him the document you have just seen yourself. He returned the next day."

"This Hagberg did?"

"Yes, Mr. Honeybath. At first Mr. Grinton blankly refused to see him again. I ventured to suggest that some slight token of civility might be in order, in the interest of international relations. So I got the Professor into Mr. Grinton's business room, and they were quite a time together. When they parted, it was cordially—very cordially indeed. Almost a puzzling thing."

"Decidedly a puzzling thing."

"And that, Mr. Honeybath, was, as I have said, some months ago. I haven't seen Professor Hagberg since."

13

WHILE APPLEBY WAS TALKING TO MISS ARNE, AND HONEY-bath to Burrow, Judith Appleby and Dolly Grinton were together making their way to the local post office. Each had discovered a need to buy stamps, and although either might have bought them for both, it had seemed companionable to make a joint expedition. The February morning was chilly, and they moved at a brisk pace. But this didn't extend to any inhibiting of conversation. Judith found Dolly sufficiently odd to be entertaining, and Dolly was disposed to admire Judith as one of not exactly trendy (which was what she tended to be herself) but at least well up in metropolitan movements in literature and the arts. Dolly read all the books that won prizes and all the theatrical notices that raved about all the new plays. Moreover there had been a Meštrovič exhibition at the Tate, with sundry exhibits brought from Zagreb and Belgrade, and as Judith was professionally equipped to pronounce upon these, a satisfactory dialogue ensued. But then suddenly— and it was of a piece with her oddity—Dolly flew off at a most unexpected tangent.

"Judith," she said, "how extraordinary it must be to have a husband who isn't *gullible!* And how *difficult!* However do you get your own way?"

"I don't know that I do." Judith decided this was an insufficiently accurate reply. "Or if I do, I never seem to notice it. Do you consider Terence to be gullible?"

"Quite exquisitely at times. But he is such a strange mixture, you see. He combines it with being more pigheaded than any man I know. Sometimes in matters that are quite important, but more frequently about things that are too small and silly for words. That chicken fund, for example."

"Oh, yes—the chicken fund. Is there really somebody who goes round giving money to old women whose chickens have been eaten by foxes?"

"Of course there is. Otherwise the old men would do something nasty to the hunting gates, and the other old men—the mounted ones, who are mostly bankers and stockbrokers far too heavy for the saddle—would come a cropper at them and break their necks. So subscriptions would fall off too."

"I see. I suppose there is a great deal of politics about fox hunting."

"The most horrid people hunt. And people even more horrid object to hunting—with banners and aniseed and heaven knows what. I sometimes wish Terence would turn civilized, and content himself with shooting pheasants and partridges, and exterminating badgers because they are bad for cows. But Terence says bugger the cows, and he isn't a bloody Hindu. Isn't it extraordinary that Terence knows about Hindus and their cows? He must have read something about them in a colour supplement."

"One does learn in surprising ways nowadays. Sometimes when I wake up early I turn on the radio and listen to the Open University. It may be about Wittgenstein or it may be about how not to bring up children. But it's always informative."

161

Dolly at once opted for Wittgenstein, being aware that he was another sacred cow. But as her knowledge of this disturbing philosopher was about equal to that of a Hindu of average accomplishment, the topic presently lapsed. The two ladies had, however, reached the post office.

So had Mrs. Mustard. Mrs. Mustard, in fact, emerged just as her hostess and fellow guest were about to enter. Although exhibiting her customary air of diffused inspiration, she somehow contrived to look agitated as well.

"*Just* in time!" she exclaimed rapidly. "A housemaid told me I could probably catch the morning collection. A most important letter to the Sadhu Nadu. We are in constant communication concerning the Further Beyond. And now I fear I must hurry on. My fixed hour for hypertranscendental meditation, you understand. Goodbye!" and Mrs. Mustard marched rapidly away.

"How very rude!" Dolly Grinton was understandably indignant. "Mightn't she have had the civility to walk back with us? And the morning collection won't be taken up for more than an hour, so she wasn't even speaking the truth. I'll tell you what! She can't bear us, and has been sending a telegram arranging for another telegram to call her urgently away. I've detected it happening at Grinton before."

Judith felt that this could be believed. She was puzzled, all the same.

"But isn't Mrs. Mustard a friend of yours?" she asked.

"Not a bit. She just wrote to me, you see. So I had a look in *Who's Who,* and they're quite respectable. She and her husband, that is. It's her husband there's a bit about—he's a professor of architecture or something, so they did seem quite okay. And I just asked her down."

"I see. What did she write to you about?"

"About there being a ghost. The Grinton Ghost. Of course old families do go in for ghosts, so it's reasonable

162

there should be a Grinton one. But I never heard of it before, and I don't like the sound of it. Live Grintons are bad enough, without dead ones on top of them."

With this harsh judgement upon her marital condition, Dolly prepared to enter the post office. But then she halted again for a moment.

"I know the stupid old woman who runs this place," she said. "She comes to the W.I. and eats my cakes at its festivities. Shall I find out from her about that telegram?"

"I think better not." Judith was quite firm. "She's not supposed to talk about other customers' business. And one oughtn't to encourage such people to do anything irregular."

"Oh, very well!"

But it was plain that Dolly Grinton considered it set a mark upon a woman to be a policeman's wife.

Charles Honeybath, meanwhile, was not easy in his mind. He felt that there was something anomalous in his having obtained from Burrow much information about Jonathan Grinton which had apparently never come the way of Jonathan's descendant Terence. It was no doubt true that the eccentricity of Terence extended to his being disposed to resent so much as a mention of those of his forbears who had trafficked in literature or the arts. But now there seemed to be a real possibility that Jonathan's affairs—or at least his luckless association with the poet Pope—had, so to speak, started alive to the extent of making an actual impact on the present state of affairs at Grinton Hall. And focal here was the mysterious Professor Hagberg. Burrow had declared that it was now some months since he had seen Professor Hagberg, and Honeybath was fairly sure that Burrow would never see Professor Hagberg again. Honeybath himself had seen him only yesterday as a dead man perched on a chair. And Terence Grinton had himself had obscure dealings with Hagberg when unprovided with information which Burrow, in his role as a family historian, could have afforded him.

So what ought Honeybath to do now? He somehow found it inconceivable that he could conduct with Terence a rational discussion of the matter; Terence, he felt, would simply roar or bellow. Very sensibly, therefore, he decided to make a beeline for Appleby and acquaint him in detail with all that had transacted itself in Burrow's pantry.

Appleby listened attentively, but gave no evidence of astonishment. It took a lot, Honeybath reflected, to astonish Appleby. Nor did Appleby announce that here, then, was at last a chink of light in darkness. It was a question less of a chink than a slot. It was as if Appleby were already in possession of a large and ordered structure into which this fresh material fitted as snugly as one could hope. So Honeybath was just a little piqued.

"I know, John," he said, "that you don't want to be too active in the mystery just because you happen to be weekending at Grinton. Perhaps I ought to have taken all this stuff to Denver."

"Denver?" Appleby seemed almost to have forgotten Denver. "Well, I don't know about that. I really don't know. Whether it's a police concern at all, that is. Not that we shan't have Denver round again before the day's out."

"Not a police concern!" Honeybath found this a most unaccountable remark. "When I actually came on a dead body . . ."

"Dead bodies are very tricky, Charles. In law, that's to say. Do you know that, if you come on a dead body and

164

believe it to be a live one, and plunge a dagger into it as a result, you can't be found guilty of attempted murder? The *mens rei* is there, of course, and that's usually quite something. But not in such a case as that. Corpses haven't much in the way of rights. Not in law."

"Body snatching," Honeybath said. "Burke and Hare."

"Hare got off—and Burke was hanged because he smothered people. Gruesome talk, Charles! But what I'm saying is that the mess we're involved with is arguably a family matter. Perhaps Terence really will be able to tell the excellent Denver to go away. And Denver would certainly be glad to be shut of us. Is that a telephone bell? What's the betting it's for me?"

And this was a good question. For it was.

"Natural causes."

"Yes, of course."

"Sir, did you hear me? That's the preliminary report on this corpse. Death from natural causes. But we shan't have a written report until tomorrow."

"All over by then. Have you been expecting to find yourself with a murder on your hands?"

"Well, sir—when somebody makes off with a dead . . ."

"Yes, yes. But murder has a smell, you know. Or an *ambience,* if that's more elegant. And this just isn't that sort of affair *at all.* I hope I don't sound dogmatic."

"Oh no, Sir John. Not in the least." Pardonably, Inspector Denver's tone betrayed a hint of sarcasm. "There's just another word or two in this interim report on the death."

"Ah!" Appleby's voice had sharpened. "Cerebral disaster—that sort of talk?"

"Approximately. Cardiac catastrophe. I suppose it means an instantaneously fatal heart attack."

"Of course it does. Any suggestion, yet, of a possible immediate predisposing cause?"

"Excitement, Sir John."

"Excitement?"

"Yes. I'd have supposed it would be the need for sudden and violent physical effort—that kind of thing. But our leech says it's often sudden emotional shock. It seems to me you wouldn't expect anything of that sort in Mr. Grinton's sleepy and deserted library."

"But it wasn't deserted, was it? Or not quite. Almost certainly at least one other person was around. And no end of persons around last night, Denver. A regular picnic."

"A regular headache, if you ask me. Just what were they all up to? The whole lot of them look to have been up to *something*."

"A very judicious observation, Inspector."

"I'm having second thoughts about that Mustard woman. I'd like to have seen a little more of what *she* was up to."

"She's been in the second-thoughts category with me too. Are you still thoroughly suspicious of Mr. Grinton himself?"

"Well no, sir. With me, he's rather been crowded out."

"Perhaps not so judicious. By the way, the corpse's name is Hagberg."

"Sir?"

"Or *was* Hagberg. I'm not sure that corpses are entitled to proper names: it's a nice theological point. Hagberg was almost certainly a professor in an American university. It would be extremely useful if you got on the line to London and had them look up all professors of that name over there. There's a reference book that gives that kind of information at once. They may find quite a clutch of Hagbergs, odd though the name be. But brief particulars will be desirable. We want a literary Hagberg, with a special interest in the eighteenth century. Can you do that?"

"Certainly I can. And I'm coming out to Grinton again after lunch."

"You'll be universally welcome, my dear fellow. Goodbye."

14

JUDITH APPLEBY, HAVING ACQUAINTED HER HUSBAND with the episode of the post office and heard the latest news of the corpse, had wandered back into the garden. Lawns had received their first mowing of the season, and pheasants were strolling on them as confidently as if they were house guests, aware that a major crisis in life was happily behind them. Rooks were already behaving industriously in great elm trees still with no hint of leaf, and virtuously drawing attention to their behaviour by producing a great deal of clamour the while. And various other natural activities were going forward.

Less natural was the behaviour of Magda Tancock, who was conscientiously playing French cricket with her children on the croquet green. It is not a particularly graceful game. The method of scoring runs, a matter of rapidly rotating the bat behind one's rump, is particularly insusceptible of aesthetically acceptable performance. Nevertheless Magda clearly regarded the entire proceeding as a callisthenic exercise, and was urging poise and rhythm upon her progeny.

"One, two, and *three*, Demetrius!" she was crying. "One, two and *three!* Florinda, dear, breathe! *Breathe!*"

"She's cheating!" Demetrius shouted furiously. "She cheated again! She counted a run when I'd already got hold of the ball. Playing with girls is stupid, stupid, stupid."

"Stupid yourself," Florinda called back. "Can't bowl me out, can't bowl me out. Cry-baby Metrius can't bowl me out!"

Thus mocked, Demetrius hurled the ball not in the direction of the bat, but of his sister's head. It was only a tennis ball, but murder was being attempted, all the same. And suddenly Magda was shouting too.

"Horrible children!" Magda shouted. "Beastly, beastly children, go away! *Go away!*" She caught herself up. "Darlings," she said, "there is dear old Mr. Mactaggart. There is grandad's dear old gardener. Run to him, sweethearts." Magda was now coaxing. "Ask Mr. Mactaggart to show you the first snowdrops. Ask him to show you"—and here Magda Tancock dived desperately into the recesses of her botanical lore—"the sweet little aconites."

"Silly snowdrops!" Florinda shouted, and stalked away in one direction.

"Bugger the aconites!" Demetrius shouted. (He had been listening to his grandfather.) And he stalked away in the other.

Charles Honeybath, had he been present, might have reflected that the *pas de deux* at Covent Garden was still a somewhat remote event on the Tancock family horizon.

"I can't think what has come over those children," Magda said, when she found that this contretemps had been observed. "It's quite unaccountable."

"Surely not." Judith was amused. "I have grandchildren who behave just like that at the drop of a handkerchief."

"I wish I'd never got married," Magda said. "Do you

know that, at Somerville, I was thought of as quite a promising scholar?"

"So you might have stayed on, and become like that formidable Miss Arne? You may have the brains, but I doubt whether you have the temperament."

"I hope that's a compliment." Magda didn't seem displeased by this piece of candour. "And perhaps I'm like my father."

Judith didn't say, "I hope not," which would have been carrying candour too far. And Magda went on at once.

"I know what it is," she said. "What makes Demetrius and Florinda so edgy today, I mean. It's Giles. Giles has gone as nervous as a cat. I suppose this dead man thing has worried him. He was quite rude to that common little Hillam at breakfast. And now he seems to want us to get away. He's even messing around with the car. And we're supposed to stay for a week. We always do."

"A couple of sunny days," Judith said, "and there will be daffodils in no time. You ought to stay for that."

This conventional remark, designed to divert Magda from uttering inappropriate criticism of her husband, was of no effect.

"And yet he's pleased with himself as well," Magda went on. "And talking about getting a Mercedes. With Eton not all that far off! It's crazy. Was Sir John at Eton?"

"He was at rather a good grammar school—level pegging with Eton, more or less. If you want an Etonian, there's Charles Honeybath. Much of a muchness with John, wouldn't you say? Two comfortable old gentlemen—just a little discomposed by what you call this dead man thing."

"I suppose my father ought to be a comfortable old gentleman too. But he never seems quite to manage it. All that bluff cheer, and hullabaloo about hounds. It's not quite all of him. A bit bewildered, don't you think? Wondering how to make do in this unaccountable day and age."

"Yesterday was certainly not without its unaccountable element. But I have a feeling it's going to be cleared up."

"I'm sure I hope so, Judith. At least I *hope* I hope so. I can't think why, but it all strikes me as rather frightening."

"I don't know why it should." Judith looked curiously at Magda Tancock. "A general malaise, perhaps, extending from your father to Demetrius and Florinda. With the exception, perhaps, of Burrow. Burrow is imperturbable. It's a *sine qua non* with butlers, and taken for granted even in advertisements. 'Wanted, an imperturbable butler.' One never sees that."

Judith offered this nonsense by way of cheering Magda up. The young woman did have a harassed air. Perhaps her husband drank, or had a vexatious habit of pestering maid-servants in corridors. Or perhaps it was just that Demetrius and Florinda were not really artistically endowed, and she knew it.

"And there *is* Giles," Magda said, "and coming this way. I expect he has a bad conscience about refusing to join in that stupid French cricket. And he has that nasty Hillam with him. Why does my mother ask such awful people down? That awful Mustard woman, for instance. A failed actress."

"Is that what Mrs. Mustard is?"

"It seems so. Burrow told me. Burrow knows everything. Long ago, she was in a play called *The Spook Sonata*. Have you ever heard of it?"

"Yes. It's by a gloomy Swede."

"It sounds like a squalid vegetable. Anyway, the play has a ghost in it, as you'd expect. And it made the woman lose her nerve, so that she never went on stage again, but took to ghosts and things on her own account. Or so Burrow

171

thinks. It's extraordinary how much Burrow thinks. Not that it prevents him from being reasonably competent. Of course he picked up his job from his father. Nobody could pick up a job from mine."

At this point Magda's husband and Hillam came up with the ladies. They had, Judith thought, a conspiratorial air. Or perhaps it wasn't quite that. Perhaps it was a kind of mutual suspicion that was between them. Probably Rosencrantz and Guildenstern distrusted one another quite a lot. So both interpretations were possible.

"Good morning," Judith said, not having seen either of the men at breakfast. "Magda thinks that mystery is bad for the children's French cricket. So I've been telling her things are clearing up."

"Not before time," Giles Tancock said. "Do you know, there are still policemen lurking around? All night, I suppose. And here still. Unobtrusively, and all that. But there they are, watching everybody's every movement. If one walked down to the village to buy a packet of cigarettes, they'd be strolling idly after you."

"It can't go on for long," Judith said—and succumbed to an impulse to venture (observantly) a little out on a limb. "They've found the body, you know."

"Found the body!" Hillam repeated with unnecessary vehemence. "All nonsense. There isn't a body. It was simply that the old dotard Honey . . ."

"Mr. Hillam," Judith said mildly.

"Oh, very well. Let there be a body." Hillam now simply sulked. "I don't give a damn."

"And just where, Lady Appleby, have they found the body?" Tancock, so worried according to his wife, appeared entirely cool. "Hauled up into an attic?"

"Somewhere in the churchyard, it seems. Among piles of bones." Judith had added this a shade inventively. "But

172

quite blamelessly dead. The throat definitely not slit from ear to ear."

"Judith, how can you be so horrid!" Magda exclaimed. "I'm sure your husband would be quite cross with you."

"Probably he would—and Mr. Denver as well. But I don't think anybody can put a foot seriously wrong, any more. Over the years, I've developed a kind of instinct in these matters. A kind of sense of smell, you know, directed upon John and his ways."

"*Really, Judith!*" Magda Tancock was yet further outraged. She appeared to feel that there had been something positively coarse in this last remark. But Judith was unabashed.

"I'm just relieving your minds," she said, "by assuring you that it will all be sewn up in the course of the day. Giles, Mr. Hillam: no need to fret. No need at all."

This impromptu incursion into nerve war on Judith's part was not without result. Hallam Hillam had gone pale, and even looked as if he were not quite in control of his knees. And Tancock was by no means unshaken, although this showed itself in the main only in a sharpened glance and a compression of the lips.

"And another thing," Judith added comfortingly. "The dead man proves to be no relation—or even, I think, friend—of anybody at Grinton. His presence here remains a little mysterious, of course, but his identity is quite clear. An American, it seems, and with an academic background. A Professor Hagberg. It's conceivable—wouldn't you say?—that he was here on some professional occasion. But we'll soon know about that too."

While this curious conversazione was going on in the garden, Charles Honeybath was engaged tête-à-tête with his host. Despite the alarms of the day and night, it seemed to him discourteous entirely to ignore what must be regarded as the more agreeable side of his visit to Grinton. He found Terence in a cubbyhole called the gunroom, engaged in what was obviously rather gloomy talk with a couple of superannuated hounds.

"I hope," Honeybath said, "we needn't let these recent troubles drive other matters entirely out of our heads. I need hardly say that I'm very keen to get on with my job."

"Your job?" As he said this, Terence glanced round the walls of the room much as if he took his visitor for an itinerant gunsmith whose services he was being solicited to retain. Then recollection came to him. "Yes, of course," he said. "My dear fellow, yes of course." Evincing by this form of words a restored sense of perfect social equality as subsisting between Honeybath and himself, Terence continued in a similarly gracious vein. "Any day," he said. "I can give you any day you choose."

"I'm afraid it must take rather more than a day." Having ceased to view Honeybath as a gunsmith, Terence was clearly thinking of him as a superior sort of photographer. "I shall want to make several sketches, for a start. And the hunting kit may be a little tricky. I could, of course, save you a bit of time by setting up a manikin, but it's something I never greatly care for."

"A manikin?" Terence seemed to sense something derogatory in being in any way associated with such a creature or object. Then he sought clearer definition. "Kind of scarecrow, eh?"

"Then there's the question of a setting." Honeybath judged it useless to pursue scarecrows and manikins further.

"By jove, yes!" Full recollection now came to Terence. "And you suggested the library. Extraordinary notion.

174

Bloody bane of my life, that place has become. I ought never to have listened to him. But he was so damned persuasive. Lucky dip idea. More like needles in haystacks, if you ask me. And that son-in-law of mine. Thinks I'm blind as a bat. Peanuts—or so I supposed, and didn't care to make a fuss. Magda wouldn't like it—and quite likely Dolly neither. But this fellow swore it was a Tom Tiddler's ground. And now corpses and constables all over the place. It confuses a man. Truth is, Honeychurch my dear chap, my mind hasn't quite the absolute clarity it used to have." Terence glanced at his watch. "But do you know? Not too early for a gin and it."

Honeybath declined this invitation (as he took it to be) and wondered whether he could venture to paint the pink-coated Terence Grinton Esquire with a wine glass of moderate size innocently in his hand. He was conscious that he had been listening to a rambling speech fragments of which, at least, were not wholly unintelligible. Perhaps he ought to hurry off and report them to Appleby. Perhaps he ought even to record that Terence had addressed him by that outlandish name of Honeychurch. Freud, after all, had shown that such slips of the tongue may be highly significant.

But Honeybath thought better of this. A coherent account of incoherence (as Freud, again, must have found) is an intellectual feat of some difficulty. And hadn't Appleby already tumbled to the entire Grinton bag of tricks? Honeybath suspected that he had.

15

"COFFEE IS SERVED IN THE LIBRARY, MADAM."

These astonishing words were uttered in a loud voice by Burrow at the end of luncheon. It may be said that two distinct astonishments inhered in them. Who ever heard of such an announcement being made in a private house at the end of a meal? And who could have dreamed of Terence Grinton's *bête noire* or White Elephant being designated for such a use?

Dolly Grinton, who had been presiding at the head of her table with her usual bright manners or mannerisms, could only suppose that Burrow had taken leave of his senses, and fear that Terence would instantly do that too. But it is essential—above all things it is essential—not to let one's husband's butler down. To reprove, or even ignore, Burrow was inconceivable. So Dolly gathered the glances of her family and guests, and charmingly exclaimed, "Shall we all go through?"

They all went through: Mr. and Mrs. Grinton, Sir John and Lady Appleby, Mr. and Mrs. Tancock, Master Tancock and Miss Tancock, Miss Arne, Mrs. Mustard, Mr. Honeybath, Mr. Hillam—and the summoning Burrow as well. They crossed the hall, walked down the long corridor, and entered the library—some achieving or affecting unconcerned chat, others silent and wondering.

And now there was something further to wonder at. Not the waiting presence of Inspector Denver (everybody might dimly have expected that), but the staggering fact that in the enormous and heraldically embellished fireplace a very sizeable fire was burning. It was a thing perfectly rational in itself; the library was by nature a chilly place, and the day remained rather chilly too; a little more warmth than small cups of coffee could generate was a thoughtful and agreeable measure. But decades, generations, conceivably even centuries had elapsed since anything of the kind was on view. So for some moments nobody had eyes for anything else.

But now another and almost equally remarkable circumstance was to be observed. The dummy door—the dummy door through which Honeybath and Appleby had passed less than twenty-four hours before—was open, uncertainly revealing the incongruously menial regions beyond. But so, too, was another dummy door, sited with a precise and wholly eighteenth-century symmetry in relation to the first. Yet the doors were not replicas the one of the other. What might be termed the Honeybath/Appleby door was masked—it will be recalled—by the mere spines of nonexistent books. The new door (although inaccurately to be so designated, since indubitably coeval with its fellow) consisted of real bookshelves supporting real books. Its construction—although by no means without precedent in similar august chambers elsewhere—evidenced considerable engineering skill on the part of the Jacobitical James Gibbs. What manner of contraption fabricated in the 1980s, it might well have been asked, is likely to be found in working order more than two hundred years on? But then James Gibbs was an ornament of his time; numerous learned monographs have been devoted to him; his working drawings are treasured in sundry public repositories devoted to the history of architecture.

Behind this notable aperture, however, lay only a small spectacle partaking of the nature of anticlimax. Everything on view lay within the depth of the circumambient wall; a few shelves, a few shallow drawers, an untidy jumble of small portfolios. Who would have thought (except, of course, the reader) that here stood revealed the very *locus arcanus* of the Grinton mystery?

"Everybody will be glad to know," Appleby said blandly as he put down his coffee cup, "that Mr. Denver, of the County Constabulary, acting with remarkable celerity, has now cleared up the difficulties arising at Grinton yesterday. Rather than embark upon explanations himself, however, he has asked me to say a word or two about the circumstances. This is because he is by no means certain that the police have any standing in the affair, and is reluctant to speak in any fashion that might seem to prejudice the official situation. May I ask, for a start, if anybody has anything to say about that?"

Nobody had—and it would not have been easy, indeed, to know how to tackle this essay in confident mystification.

"Mr. Grinton's family," Appleby went on, "is fully represented here—as it ought to be when we are considering what is essentially a family concern. As for the venue, it has occurred to Mr. Grinton and myself that this beautiful library is the right place, since matters must arise in which a view of its precise layout will be advantageous to a ready comprehension of one or two matters I must mention."

Appleby paused on this, as if to hint that there was no

particular need for haste in achieving the small elucidation before him. For a moment it seemed that Terence Grinton was prompted to speech—probable to deny that anything had occurred to him at all. He looked searchingly around the room instead, perhaps in the hope of discovering that Burrow had thought to back up the coffee with a supply of brandy. Burrow, however, was merely circling the company with a salver from which more coffee, cream and sugar were on offer. Having accomplished this, he took up an unobtrusive station at the rear of the assembly, after the fashion in which functionaries of his order resign themselves to sitting out (or standing out) the eloquence traditionally following upon a banquet.

"For a start," Appleby said, "I must ask you to bear with me while I say a word about what, in a court of law, might be described as the two principal documents in the case. I shall have to emphasize, incidentally, that there is a radical difference between them.

"We must begin, strangely enough, by carrying our minds back to the middle of the seventeenth century, and considering the career and personality of a certain Ambrose Grinton, who flourished during the period of the Restoration. Our authority here is a book called *Reliquiae Grintonianae*, compiled by a certain Simon Upcott within a century of Ambrose's death. It was privately printed and is no doubt very scarce, although there will almost certainly be copies in the great national libraries. And one copy, which I have had the advantage of consulting, is in the possession of Mr. Burrow, Mr. Grinton's butler. The relevant facts we learn from it are these: Ambrose travelled in France and Italy; he was interested in the fine arts; he was a collector, not always of too scrupulous a habit; and in Rome he acquired, and presumably brought home, a substantial collection of drawings and watercolours by Claude Lorrain. These have never been heard of since. If discovered, they would be worth a very large sum of money.

"So much, for the moment, for Ambrose Grinton. We come now to Jonathan Grinton—Ambrose's grandson, as I suppose him to have been. Jonathan's interest lay in literature, and he was even something of a writer himself: only half an hour ago, Miss Arne was good enough to tell me that in 1715 he published a book called *Divers Private Recreations,* no copy of which appears to have survived. He also kept a journal. For many years it seems to have lain hidden in this very library. But eventually—no doubt during renovations or the like—it was destroyed."

At this point in his expository effort, Appleby paused and glanced at Terence Grinton. But Terence again had nothing to say. He may well have been totally at sea amid all this antiquarian matter.

"Fortunately," Appleby resumed, "certain excerpts from Jonathan's journal had been made by Mr. Burrow, who takes an informed and—if I may say so—scholarly interest in the Grinton family. They show that Jonathan himself owned a lively pen—and also, perhaps, that something of his temperament has been inherited by at least one later Grinton. What we learn from one of these excerpts is this: Alexander Pope, while still a very young man but already of some celebrity as a poet, was entertained by Jonathan here at Grinton; the two men fell out and there was something of a violent quarrel; Pope was expelled from the house, or at least left in a hurry—but not before he had composed a virulent satire (as we may suppose it to have been) upon Grinton and the Grintons. This satire he virtually flung at Jonathan, apparently as a hint of what he might one day commit to print. This he never did But Jonathan preserved—here in this library, he actually asserts—what he regarded as a criminal composure, thinking in some hazy way that it might on some future occasion afford useful evidence of the dastardly nature of the young poet's character.

"And now to that difference between the Ambrose record and the Jonathan one. Of the probable continued existence here of the Claude drawings and paintings there is evidence for anybody who happens upon a copy of *Reliquiae Grintonianae*. Of the existence—and the probable continued existence—of the Pope satire there is no evidence whatever except that preserved in Mr. Burrow's purported transcript."

"*Sir!*" Burrow exclaimed.

"I do beg your pardon, Mr. Burrow." For the first time, Appleby spoke with strong emphasis. "It is, in the first place, a purely legalistic point. Only if we are all unhappily landed in court is there the slightest likelihood of the integrity of your testimony being challenged. But the material fact is this: your transcript from Jonathan Grinton's journal is the only channel through which Pope's satire can have come within the notice of anybody. And that brings us to Professor Hagberg—unfortunately the late Professor Hagberg."

"*Hagberg!*" Terence Grinton produced this as a kind of alarmed shout. It might almost have been said that he had turned pale, like some Shelleyan abstraction that hears pronounced the dreaded name of Demogorgon. "Hasn't the fellow cleared out? Damned awkward thing. Not quite aboveboard, perhaps. But these are devilish hard times, you know."

"He certainly hasn't cleared out in the sense you intend."

Appleby seemed unsurprised by the deepening incoherence of his host. "The body in this library was Hagberg's, without a doubt. But before discussing that, let us pause for a moment to clarify our ground so far. We have to conceive of the presence, here at Grinton, of two totally distinct lures or prizes: a batch of minor works by Claude Lorrain, and a hitherto unknown and unsuspected satire by Alexander Pope. They are by no means prizes of equal monetary value, but Professor Hagberg—to come back to him— would certainly have preferred to stumble on the poem rather than the pictures. He was a prime authority on Pope—so Mr. Denver has discovered with his admirable expedition—and he came to Grinton in the first place simply because of Pope's known association with the house. I have, of course, no doubt that Mr. Grinton received him with complete civility . . ."

"Rubbish!" Giles Tancock interrupted rudely. "The old ruffian would have kicked him through the door."

"But unquestionably"—Appleby continued, disregarding this—"the professor experienced a sense of impasse. He was, in fact, discomfited, and his discomfiture was remarked by Mr. Burrow. Mr. Burrow has a high regard for the amenities, and particularly as they should be pursued at Grinton. He therefore entertained the professor in his own part of the house. And being aware, as a consequence of his extensive studies, of the professor's overriding interest as an English scholar, he afforded him a view of the transcript to which I have referred. This was only a few months ago. And from then until this very day, Mr. Burrow and Professor Hagberg were presumably the only people in the world to have heard of this particular satire by Alexander Pope."

Appleby paused for a moment, as if deliberating with

182

himself how best to proceed. He was at least assured of the entire attention of his auditory. Dolly Grinton had ceased being bright, and had an apprehensive look. Miss Arne was concentrating upon what she heard just as she must have concentrated in her time upon hundreds and hundreds of disquisitions by pupils less accomplished than the retired Commissioner of Police. Mrs. Mustard, although presumably much occupied with the Further Beyond, was nervously chewing her nails. All the gentlemen, including Burrow, looked as if they had plenty to think about. Even Demetrius and Florinda, although provided with pencil and paper for the purpose of quarrelsome games of noughts and crosses, were gazing at Appleby openmouthed.

"Presumably as a result of his exciting meeting with Mr. Burrow," Appleby resumed, "Professor Hagberg returned to Grinton on the following day, and had what appears to have been a more fruitful discussion with Mr. Grinton. But to just what effect, I confess myself to being a little in the dark. So it will be very helpful to us if, at this stage, Mr. Grinton will tell us about it. Terence, would that be agreeable to you?"

For a moment it didn't look as if it would be at all agreeable. Terence muttered something about confounded nonsense and sending for his solicitor. Appleby murmured in turn his conviction that all this was merely a family affair and a private one at that.

"Oh, very well," Terence said. "Great confidence in you, John. Vast experience, and all that. So here it is."

"Hagberg," Terence Grinton said, "appeared out of the blue. He knew nothing about this satire thing we've been hearing about. What he was after was letters. Letters written in historical times, at that. Did you ever hear such nonsense? Who would keep letters about the Spanish Armada and the Norman Conquest and so forth? And he was on about this Pope—so where were they? Hagberg seemed to think I'd have them right at hand, like the bills Burrow brings along from the butcher and baker. Of course, John, I was completely civil, as you rightly say. I just told him to bugger off."

"And he did?" Appleby asked.

"Yes—and I knew nothing about his having a little chat with Burrow. No reason why he should not, if he had a fancy that way. But the next day he was back again, and singing to a different tune. Switched scents, you might say. He said he had a great deal of sympathy for the plight of the English landed classes, and that he had an ancestor who knew George Washington. It seems that Washington came of very decent people in Northamptonshire. Getting on for the best of the Shires, to my mind. Tiptop hunting country."

At this point Terence seemed in some danger of losing his thread, and had to be prompted by Appleby.

"And just what," Appleby asked, "did Hagberg propose to do about the plight of the landed classes?"

"He said that if you were hard up you looked around for this and that to sell in an unobtrusive way. I knew what he meant, of course. Capital Gains Tax. I have some piece of rubbish—say an old Chinese chamberpot or the like—and you flog it to some lunatic for thousands of pounds. Then along comes a tax blighter and filches the cash from you. So softly, softly was the thing, he said. And particularly with books. There was probably no end of books scattered around this library that were worth a packet. He quite surprised me."

"And he offered to find them and feed them quietly on

the market?" Appleby thought it injudicious to modify Terence's view on the operations of the tax man. "Perhaps for a trifling commission?"

"Just that. Quite a businesslike chap, really. But it all had to be thoroughly hush-hush. He oughtn't to be seen regularly coming and going at Grinton. So he thought of this ploy. Camping on the scene of operations, you might say. Ingenious idea, eh? And with quite a bit of spunk to it. I liked that." At this point Terence chuckled happily. "Not even Burrow would know about it. And Burrow knows about damn nearly everything. That right, Burrow?"

"I endeavour to keep in touch, sir."

"Well, there you are. It would all take time, Hagberg said. A lot of poking around to do."

"Decidedly," Appleby said.

"And the next thing, the blasted man has gone dead on us. And what he has been after all the time is this confounded satire. Found it, too, if I understand what you've been saying, John. And I've been following you very closely—very closely indeed. It needs a clear head. But I've never been short of that, thank God."

Terence Grinton sat back, having manfully done his duty. Either because impressed or because stupefied, the assembled company was momentarily silent. And then Appleby spoke again.

"So far as the satire goes," he said, "—but don't forget about Claude—there is only one other preliminary trail to follow. It concerns Mr. Grinton's son-in-law, Mr. Giles Tancock. What nobody had any notion of, except perhaps in a dim way Mr. Grinton himself, is that Mr. Tancock too was interested in the books in this library. Just as a matter of family entitlement, you might say, he had fallen into the habit of removing a useful-looking volume every now and then. As a matter of fact, it appears that he became quite systematic about it. He knows about books; all the antiquarian booksellers' catalogues come to him; he found them useful as a guide to what to look out for. Mr. Tancock, would you care to confirm me in this?"

"Not in so far as it suggests a misrepresentation." Tancock, who had gone pale, said this very carefully. "You ought to have stressed that my father-in-law knew about it. I suppose he was aware that I am as hard up as he is. And— to put it crudely—he didn't want a rumpus. He's scared of the women, you know. He's that sort of chap."

"It's not, perhaps, a line of inquiry we need pursue further at the moment." Appleby said this a shade grimly. "For we have arrived at a crucial moment yesterday afternoon. Mr. Tancock makes one of his predatory visits to this room. He finds Professor Hagberg—of whose existence he has known nothing—in it. The professor has Pope's satire—of which, again, Mr. Tancock knows nothing—in his hands. And the professor is dead."

This time, the silence was prolonged. It was Appleby himself who broke it.

"And now," Appleby said. "we can turn to Claude Lorrain. Two of the present small house party at Grinton are here solely because of him. In fact they got themselves severally invited down simply in the hope of getting a sight of Ambrose Grinton's little collection. Or at least let us express it like that just for the moment. And remember that the continued existence here at Grinton of these valuable works of art might be inferred by anybody who had happened upon one of those rare copies of *Reliquiae Grintonianae.* One of the two was Mr. Hallam Hillam."

"It's a lie!" Hillam said—or, rather, shouted. "It's a disgusting fabrication, and most certainly an actionable slander."

"Mr. Hillam," Appleby continued, unheeding, "is by profession an art historian. He presumably came on the book in the course of research into connoisseurship in England in the seventeenth century. To act on the information it gave was decidedly to take a long shot, and Mr. Hillam may well have been rather despondent about his enterprise. But then he came upon a little Claude watercolour hanging amazingly on the drawing room wall. That must have cheered him up no end. But of course he can have had very little notion how to proceed. He knew about the deserted and disorganized state of this library, and if the bulk of the drawings were anywhere they were probably here. But as to just where, he had no information at all. It was otherwise with Mrs. Mustard.

"Mrs. Mustard, incidentally, is an actress." Appleby hadn't paused. "She has retired from the stage—although whether it has really been in favour of spiritual pursuits, I don't know. In the theatre, I can hardly doubt that she had a distinguished career. Her profession, however, is of less significance than that of her husband. For here another professor enters our story. Professor Mustard's subject is the history of English architecture, and in the course of his researches he undoubtedly came upon James Gibbs's working drawings for a library at Grinton Hall. Gibbs was a Classical man. He believed in symmetry—not fearful, as in William Blake's celebrated poem, but comfortable and at times unobtrusive. *Grove nods at grove, each alley has a brother,* as Pope himself somewhere has it. And the same thing should go even for concealed doors. So we can be sure that his drawing for this library reveals just what you

187

are looking at now. There, in fact, in that masked cup-board, was a convenient repository either for junk or treas-ure. Just where the Claudes had knocked around in Am-brose's time, we don't know. But it wasn't a bad bet that this was where they now reposed. Jonathan Grinton, for example, may have been a little uncomfortable about his grandfather's depredations in Rome, and may have shoved some of his loot into this whimsical hidey hole. So you can see that Mrs. Mustard was a long way ahead of Mr. Hillam."

After this long speech, Appleby, very reasonably, paused to take breath. This gave Mrs. Mustard, hitherto silent, an opportunity to participate in the discussion.

"*Woe!*" Mrs. Mustard cried aloud. "*Woe to profane inquirers into forbidden things!*"

"Yes, indeed," Appleby said. "A good deal of discomfort is likely to result. And I must apologize for the tedium of this preliminary exposition. But at least we are arrived at the point at which action begins."

16

DURING THESE EXPLANATIONS, CHARLES HONEYBATH HAD found himself glancing from time to time at the fire now blazing on the hearth. He had been visited by a new and rather wonderful idea. That vision of depicting the proprietor of Grinton as posed before a towering array of books had been entirely fantastic. Terence wouldn't have stood for it for a moment. But here was the library in comfortable (or perhaps uncomfortable) use again. So why not have him toasting his behind in front of this cheerful conflagration? It was the technical aspect of this that was extremely alluring. That hunting pink—and then the flickering crimson and orange and gold and mere incandescence behind it: would it be possible to bring that off? Honeybath felt impatient— anxious that Appleby would hasten his winding up of the tiresome business of the disappearing Professor Hagberg and permit more serious business to get going. Fortunately Appleby did now seem to be proposing a brisk pace.

"So there are two perfectly definite occasions to cope with," Appleby was saying. "The first concerns what happened in this library and elsewhere yesterday afternoon, and the second what happened here in the middle of the night.

"Let me begin with the bizarrely squatting Hagberg. Here he is, pretending to be assembling likely books for the improving of Mr. Grinton's bank balance, but actually on the hunt for Alexander Pope's satire. Remember that he hasn't a clue as to where it may be lurking. He has been down in the basement—where he has presumably been often enough before—and the only result has been his getting smothered in dust and cobweb. He retires to that little room for modest physical recruitment. And then, halfway through the discussion of a Welsh Rabbit, and like the boy in Browning's poem, he is stung by the splendour of a sudden thought. It is a moment of tremendous excitement. He, too, is a Classical man. And there has come to him, more or less intuitively, the probability—the near necessity—of the existence of that symmetrical door and hiding place." And here Appleby paused, and pointed with a muted dramatic gesture. "There it is, and within minutes he has spotted it and opened it. He rummages, perhaps for quite some time. And then Pope's satire is in his hands.

"He shuts the door—if door it's to be called—and stands there reading the thing. It's tremendous. As sheer malign attack, it's tremendous. He rejoices in it, and his features betray the fact. Then, quite suddenly, he is dead. He suffers from what his compatriots call a condition—meaning a disease. He's taking pills for it. But it strikes, and there he is: dead as a doornail, huddled on the floor. No more than a few minutes pass, and Mr. Tancock enters the library."

It was decidedly a shocked silence this time. Terence Grinton stood up, moved across the room, and actually placed himself with his back to the fire, as if a chill sense of mortality could be mitigated that way.

"Mr. Tancock's resulting behaviour," Appleby went on,

"is distinctly interesting. Simultaneously, or at least in rapid alternation, he may be said to keep his head and lose it. He doesn't know Hagberg from Adam. The thing is totally inexplicable. But then he picks up Pope's manuscript—which we may suppose to be on several sheets scattered on the floor—and discovers what it is almost at once. Here is something of high literary interest, and of considerable value as well."

"*Considerable?*" Rather surprisingly, Miss Arne found herself with a contribution to make. "A few months ago, fifty-seven lines of *The Revolt of Islam* in Shelley's own hand was sold at Sotheby's for over nine thousand pounds."

"Nine thousand pounds!" This came from Terence in a kind of agonized shout. "For a wretched piece of scribbling: nine thousand pounds!"

"A complete work by Pope, in his own hand and hitherto unknown," Miss Arne said crisply, "would certainly fetch much more than that."

"So you will see," Appleby resumed, "how things stood. Mr. Tancock had no notion that Hagberg was in the library with his father-in-law's connivance. He supposed him to be a simple thief, but one whose sudden death could decidedly be put to account. In short, Mr. Tancock pocketed the manuscript. It was not for nothing, we may say, that he had married into the family of Autolycus Grinton. So now he was in high spirits, and prompted to do a singularly freakish thing. He emptied the dead man's pockets, perched the body on a chair, and left the library as he had entered it; by the door, that is to say, by which we have ourselves come in. He may thereby narrowly have escaped encountering Mr. Honeybath, who himself entered the room a few minutes later.

"It will be convenient to continue following Mr. Tancock

for the moment. Retreating, perhaps to his own room, he examines the personal belongings of the dead man he has brought away with him. He thus discovers the dead man's name, and at once his position is transformed. He knows that a Professor Hagberg is an authority on Pope, and that if his identity is discovered much inquiry must follow. So it is essential to remove the body. He returns to the library— this time unobtrusively by the bogus door from the rear of the building—carts the body out to his car, and makes off with it to what he conceives of as a brilliant temporary hiding place. It is now that Mr. Honeybath returns to the library, accompanied by myself. To Mr. Honeybath's considerable confusion, there is no dead body to be found.

"We search the library, discover the bogus door, discover the little room with its unaccountable temporary furnishings, return to the library, lock it up, and withdraw. Mr. Tancock meanwhile returns from the churchyard, proposing to reenter the house through the deserted domestic offices. He chances to glance into the little room, and realizes the purpose to which it has been put. But he still, you must remember, believes that nobody knows anything about the whole affair except himself. So these further traces of mysterious activity must be removed too. He bundles the camp bed and everything else into his car, returns to the church with them, dumps them in the vestry, and drives back to Grinton. We are not yet quite finished with Mr. Tancock, since there is something he has been careless about. We are finished, however, with the events of the afternoon. The events of the night are to follow."

"But quite a lot more happened yesterday afternoon." Dolly Grinton broke in with this rather as if accused of having provided insufficient entertainment for her guests.

"We all heard about Mr. Honeybath finding a body, and Terence told me to send for Mr. Denver, and statements were taken, and goodness knows what."

"Perfectly true," Appleby said. "But the next active moves came from Mr. Hillam and Mrs. Mustard, when the rest of us had all gone to bed. Not that 'the rest of us' includes Mr. Denver and his men. They were lurking in this library and very much awake.

"So consider Mr. Hillam and Mrs. Mustard a little more closely. They know nothing about Pope. But they are competing, as it were, for the Claudes, each ignorant of the designs of the other. But it isn't a competition on equal terms. Mr. Hillam has only a vague notion that the booty is probably somewhere here in the library. Come to think of it, his is rather a forlorn hope. He is here merely for a long weekend, and what can he really do about it? The Claude he has detected hanging in the drawing room makes his position only the more tantalizing. One almost sympathizes with Mr. Hillam and his ill-concealed irritation and bafflement. However, he is a predatory person, betraying the hospitality extended to him. And that goes for Mrs. Mustard too."

"I declare Sir John Appleby," Mrs. Mustard said firmly, "to be diabolically possessed. His is one of the most striking cases with which I have met."

"Mrs. Mustard holds a big advantage over Mr. Hillam. She knows about that capacious secret cupboard, into which anything awkward or inconvenient or even confidential is likely to have been stuffed from time to time. Mrs. Mustard is simply waiting for a good opportunity to explore it.

"But now circumstances have suddenly altered: the mysterious body, policemen all over the place. Mrs. Mustard decides she must act. So does Mr. Hillam. And so—to come back to him—does Mr. Tancock. It has been Mr. Tancock's habit to pursue his researches in the library with the help of a batch of antiquarian bookseller's catalogues. But one of these he finds to be missing. He decides he must have left it in the basement (where, in fact, I myself came on it earlier in the day) and that the situation is a dodgy one. The catalogue may well be found and occasion undesirable speculation. He may even imagine his own fingerprints as on it: that sort of thing. Fingerprints are much in the minds of the laity when criminal matters are in question. And now it becomes known—or, rather, believed—that the police have vacated the library. So Mr. Tancock comes downstairs in the small hours and descends into that basement.

"Then comes Mrs. Mustard. She brings with her in a bag some of the standard paraphernalia of spiritualistic séances: they will serve for obfuscation should she be detected. The lurking police are invisible. So, as she moves about, is she for appreciable periods to the police. She finds that massively disguised cupboard, opens it, rummages, quickly comes on the small portfolio containing the Claudes, stuffs it in her bag, and closes the door. It is in that very moment, I imagine, that in comes Mr. Hillam. Mr. Hillam is, you know, rather an ineffective person. He starts a useless and dangerous row with the lady. And at this point Mr. Tancock—if one may so express it—surfaces.

"One can, incidentally, a little enter into Mr. Tancock's state of mind. He hasn't found the catalogue, so that remains a minor worry. A far bigger one is the fact that his plan to remove all trace of Professor Hagberg's presence has miscarried, and that he has, quite crazily, landed himself with a very awkward situation at the church. On the other hand he has the unexpected windfall of the satire and no notion that it is in anybody else's mind. A big reward for his efforts is, therefore, still possible. But he will need all his wits if he is to extricate himself from the fix in which he finds himself.

"So there is last night's total situation—apart from Mr. Grinton's turning up and firing a revolver, and so forth. There really isn't much mystery left."

Perhaps unexpectedly, it was Magda Tancock who first collected herself in face of this doubtless-elucidated but nevertheless, uncomfortable situation.

"At least Giles has that satire," she said, "although he has behaved a little oddly about it. That's just, as Sir John has said, a family affair, and to be put right accordingly. I've been worried about all this, and now I know why." Magda turned quickly to her children. "My darlings," she said, "are you having such a nice, nice game?"

Florinda failed to respond to this maternal solicitude. Demetrius put out his tongue. But since he was a polite child, it was at his sister and not his mother.

"But what about the Claudes?" It was Hillam who demanded this, and he was glaring vindictively at Mrs. Mustard. "Of course I haven't been involved at all. I've explained that. But this damned woman must be made to hand them over. And then she must be put in gaol."

"I'm afraid that must be rather doubtful," Appleby said, "and I think Mr. Denver will agree with me. I don't believe the pictures are any longer in the lady's possession. And—what's more important—I much doubt whether they could legally be proved ever to have been so. I've offered, you know, only what can be called a conjecture. Suppose it to be true. What will the lady have done? Hurried to the local post office, I'd say, and despatched them to an unknown destination. Suppose that they turn up later—on an American market, perhaps, in six months' time. How is Mr. Grinton going to prove that they were ever in his ownership, or to be identified with the Claudes mentioned in that gossipy *Reliquiae Grintonianae?* It would be a cockeyed case from the start. In fact, it's most unlikely that Mrs. Mustard will be required to pursue her transcendental meditations in prison, although she certainly deserves to do so."

"And what about the satire?" Giles Tancock suddenly spoke up boldly. "What proof is there that it in any sense passed into the possession of Jonathan Grinton, or that it was written in this house or remained in this house? Jonathan Grinton's Journal? There's no proof that anything of the sort ever existed. There's nothing but that so-called transcript, made by my father-in-law's creature, Burrow."

"Ladies and gentlemen," Burrow said, "I respectfully beg you to take note of what has just been said. I have the penalties attached to slanderous utterance in mind."

"And it won't wash, Mr. Tancock." Inspector Denver, hitherto silent, had risen and advanced to the centre of the room. "There will be no doubt, you know, about that body having been in your car. Our forensic people are seeing to that. Legally, mind you, your dealings with the dead Hagberg may be on the tricky side. I can imagine counsel representing that, not wishing to cause distress in a weekend party, you quietly removed the body *pro tem* to holy ground. Nonsense of that sort. But, taking one thing with another, your prospects aren't good. Unless you act quietly in a family way."

"And hand over that Pope thing!" Terence Grinton said— or, rather, produced as a shout. "I'm told I've lost those daubs by Claude Whatshisname, and an enormous sum of

196

money as a result. But I'll bloody well have the poem. Nine thousand pounds! Hand it over, blast you!"

And Giles Tancock gave in. Reluctantly, he put a hand in an inner pocket. Reluctantly, he produced a sheaf of yellowed papers and handed them to his father-in-law.

"Then there you are," he said. "And much good they do you."

Terence plainly thought they were going to do him quite a lot of good—thousands of pounds of it, so mad was the world. He stared at the papers, at first unbelievingly and then—it seemed—with a certain stirring of curiosity. What on earth could be the sort of tosh that people would give that money for?

Terence turned over a page, and read. He actually *read:* there could be no doubt about it. And as he read, his brow darkened. His brow darkened, his face flushed. His face turned red beyond (it might have been said) the scope of Charles Honeybath's palette. And then he uttered a roar of rage. Totally inarticulate at first, it swiftly revealed itself as imprecation of no common order. Terence was on the verge of apoplectic seizure. Offering in energetic heroic couplets his estimate of Grinton and the Grintons, the metrical death adder Alexander Pope looked to be at work again. Mr. Grinton was as Professor Hagberg had been, but with furious indignation taking the place of glee.

And then it was all over. With a final bellow of fury, Terence crumpled the manuscript and hurled it into the heart of the fire. Nine thousand pounds was something. But the honour of the Grintons was something more.

Everybody looked on, stunned. Nobody knew what to say. Or nobody except Judith Appleby. Judith glanced at her watch and turned to Dolly.

"Why, Dolly!" she said. "It's almost teatime."

So they all dispersed. Or all except Terence Grinton, who remained staring at the fire, and Charles Honeybath, who advanced upon him with quiet resolution.

"Grinton," Honeybath said, "I think we should perhaps give our minds to the question of the portrait."

"The portrait?" For a moment Terence was understandably a little at sea. And then he remembered.

"Yes, of course," he said. "My dear fellow, yes, of course. Wednesday or Thursday—or any day you like."

200